ONE NIGHT WITH YOU

MONTGOMERY INK LEGACY
BOOK 7

CARRIE ANN RYAN

One Night WITH YOU

CARRIE ANN

NEW YORK TIMES BESTSELLING AUTHOR

RYAN

One Night With You

A Montgomery Ink Legacy Romance

By: Carrie Ann Ryan

© 2024 Carrie Ann Ryan

Cover Art by Sweet N Spicy Designs

All content warnings are listed on the book page for this book on my website.

PRAISE FOR CARRIE ANN RYAN

"Count on Carrie Ann Ryan for emotional, sexy, character driven stories that capture your heart!" – Carly Phillips, NY Times bestselling author

"Carrie Ann Ryan's romances are my newest addiction! The emotion in her books captures me from the very beginning. The hope and healing hold me close until the end. These love stories will simply sweep you away." ~ NYT Bestselling Author Deveny Perry

"Carrie Ann Ryan writes the perfect balance of sweet and heat ensuring every story feeds the soul." - Audrey Carlan, #1 New York Times Bestselling Author

"Carrie Ann Ryan never fails to draw readers in with passion, raw sensuality, and characters that pop off the page. Any book by Carrie Ann is an absolute treat." – New York Times Bestselling Author J. Kenner

"Carrie Ann Ryan knows how to pull your heart-strings and make your pulse pound! Her wonderful Redwood Pack series will draw you in and keep you reading long into the night. I can't wait to see what comes next with the new generation, the Talons. Keep them coming, Carrie Ann!" –Lara Adrian, New York Times bestselling author of CRAVE THE NIGHT

"With snarky humor, sizzling love scenes, and brilliant, imaginative worldbuilding, The Dante's Circle series reads as if Carrie Ann Ryan peeked at my personal wish list!" – NYT Bestselling Author, Larissa Ione

"Carrie Ann Ryan writes sexy shifters in a world full of passionate happily-ever-afters." – *New York Times* Bestselling Author Vivian Arend

"Carrie Ann's books are sexy with characters you can't help but love from page one. They are heat and heart blended to perfection." *New York Times* Bestselling Author Jayne Rylon

Carrie Ann Ryan's books are wickedly funny and deliciously hot, with plenty of twists to keep you guessing. They'll keep you up all night!" USA Today Bestselling Author Cari Quinn

"Once again, Carrie Ann Ryan knocks the Dante's Circle series out of the park. The queen of hot, sexy, enthralling paranormal romance, Carrie Ann is an author not to miss!" *New York Times* bestselling Author Marie Harte

To the ones who thought they were nothing. Who were told that they were always the best friend. The funny one. The ones that were told to get out of the way. The ones who thought nobody saw them.

We see you.

I see you.

You deserve your happiness.

You've earned it.

PROLOGUE
CLAIRE

Dear Diary,

I used to write about my hopes and dreams. About the crush I had on a friend of a friend. I used to write about the man I wanted to be mine —if he could only see me.

I used to write about so many things.

But now I only see the darkness.

And I don't know what I'm supposed to do with that.

I don't want to write anymore. I just want to live and find a way to be free.

So that's why I walked away from the man I loved.

Because it wasn't his fault he didn't see me.

I want to find my own happiness.
I want to find my own forever.
I just want to be safe.
Only I don't know how I can.
Not anymore.
-Claire

1

KINGSTON

T here were some days where it felt as if you were on top of the world. Where nothing you could do would be wrong. You hit every green light. You were always the first one at a four-way stop. If you needed to go by train or light rail, you would never miss a stop, and would always find the best place to sit. You would get the most perfectly ripe pineapple at the grocery store. The ones that were perfectly sweet, and yet not too soft. And then you could also get the avocado that was a little firm when you first got it that morning, but as soon as you needed it that evening, it was perfectly ripened.

There were some days where your life just made sense. And nothing could go wrong.

And then there were days where you were knee-deep in what had to be some form of dog excrement, looking up at the gutters you had slightly fallen from, wondering exactly where life had gone wrong.

"You okay down there, Kingston?"

I glared up at my cousin Kane and wondered exactly when my life had taken just such a drastic turn.

He was still safely on the ladder, while I knew I'd be covered in mud—and whatever else—for the rest of my life. There was no way I was going to get it out of every crevice it had seemed to sink into.

Because it wasn't that I had just fallen off the ladder. No. I had been *pushed*. Not by my cousin—by the German shepherd that had been the previous security for this tenant.

Apparently, he didn't like the fact that I was taking over his job.

I owned Montgomery Security with my family. We did numerous types of jobs around the city. Whether it was bodyguard services, potential layouts for large corporations in security, or planning for those security systems. We did a little bit of everything—including adding security systems to homes. Like this home, which had used a German shepherd as its security for so long that apparently this four-legged adorable doofus who could bite me at any minute didn't appreciate the change.

Today however this lovely German shepherd named

Bosley had decided my ladder needed to be taken down a peg. Or rather I did. So now I was knee-deep in this mud pit after the lovely Colorado rain, staring at Bosley.

"Should I be looking him in the eyes? He is not a golden retriever. He's a German shepherd. He could bite my face off."

"He's not going to bite your face off," Kane answered while clearly holding back a laugh, as he slowly made his way down his ladder.

Ford, our co-owner and my cousin-in-law, gave me a sigh as he walked around the building. "What did I say about playing in the mud?"

It wasn't only mud, but I wasn't in the mood to explain that. "That I should do it with more vigor?"

"Come on, Bosley. Let's go for a walk."

Bosley tilted his head as he stared at me, even though he seemed quite interested in Ford's words.

"Walk," Ford repeated, and Bosley scampered off to go see his new best friend, while I tried to get out of the mud pit.

"I just bought these jeans," I grumbled, as I slid once again, slamming my knee into the ground. "Fuck," I muttered under my breath, grateful the owner wasn't here to witness this.

Oh yes, top-notch security and professionalism. Me rolling around in damn mud because they had decided to leave their dog in the backyard rather in the house where they'd said they would. I liked dogs and wanted one of my own. But this one was a little rambunctious and didn't listen to all commands. Bosley was headed back to training so he could provide a sense of safety for others, but he was just a little young and a little wild as of yet—hence why he'd knocked me off my ladder. We were almost done with the installation, and now I needed a damn shower.

"I've got a towel in the truck."

I raised a brow at Kane. "Why do you have a towel in the truck?"

"In case it rained," my best friend and cousin said, as if it made all the difference.

I just shook my head and toed off my boots so I wouldn't drag mud splotches all over the pavement and stone pathway the owners had put in. So now in my socked feet, I tiptoed my way to the truck. Kane had graciously unlocked it for me, and I found the towel on the back seat before trying to wipe off some of the mud. It became this cakey substance, and I definitely smelled dog shit.

Great.

Great.

I'd had a shitty month. Hell, I'd had a shitty six months. Everything that I seemed to do these days turned to ash. *Literally* in some cases. I was just too tired these days from watching things that I wanted to happen fall through.

Whether it was dates, plans, or even household issues.

I'd moved in the past few months because the place I had been sharing with Kane no longer worked for our situation. Considering Kane was now happily with Phoebe, and they were ready to start their lives and forever and all that bullshit. Meaning we all needed space. So I had a new place that needed work. Apparently saying that I wanted a fixer-upper meant I got one. It didn't help that some of my family was in the construction business. So they all wanted to help, and could do it better than me, but I had wanted to try it myself.

And that meant everything was taking longer than it should. I just needed to get over myself and let them help.

I pulled off my shirt in the middle of the driveway and tugged a clean one on. I had extra pants, but I wasn't about to get naked in here. I would just have to sit on a towel and shower when I got back to the office. Thankfully the security setup was almost done, and Ford would put the dog back in the house where he needed to be, and we would get back home.

I just wanted my house to fix itself, I wanted little things at work not to turn into big things like they seemed to these days, and I wanted Claire to answer my calls.

I frowned at my thoughts, knowing Claire ignoring me was the source of my problems lately.

Claire Harlow.

Phoebe's best friend, and a thorn in my paw.

It really wasn't her fault, but it was. She had been hurt a few months back when Phoebe's stalker, and a man that had wanted to hurt our family, had taken both Claire and Phoebe hostage. It was something that happened in my line of work far too often. Not our friends being attacked per se, but violent people were in our lives, and it was our job to protect those around us. We were the ones who stopped things like this from happening. That was why we were Montgomery Security. But we hadn't been able to stop that man from hurting Phoebe and Claire.

Claire had been *stabbed* in the process.

I could still feel the sticky blood on my palms as I had held Claire's side, keeping the wound sealed as much as possible, telling her that everything would be okay, even though I felt as if I were lying to myself and her.

I could still see her reflection in the mirror when she had been staring at her stitched-upside and looking far more lost than I'd ever seen her.

Claire was a pistol. She had come into our lives

because Phoebe and Kane started dating, and because Kane and I were best friends, Claire and I hung out. She was quiet, but nice. Always had good jokes and could make everyone at the table laugh unexpectedly.

And then she moved out of the apartment she shared with Phoebe to find her own place because Phoebe and Kane were going to move in together.

I had failed to protect her. I had failed to keep her safe. And all I really wanted to do was keep her safe.

I wanted to make sure she was okay because I hadn't liked what I had seen in that mirror. But she hadn't let me take care of her.

"Not friends? Fuck that," I muttered to myself.

She had laughed when I had said we were friends. At least I thought we had been. But maybe we had just been friends of friends, and those connections didn't matter. But now here I was, grumbly like a bear, on one of my last days of work before I was taking a damn vacation.

What was I supposed to do with myself?

"Why do you look like you're having a very deep and angry conversation in your head right now?" Kane asked.

I scowled since he'd not only read me correctly, I'd also been talking to myself. "Can we just get me back to the office. I need a shower. And then I have a meeting with Hudson."

"Oh yeah. Today's tattoo prep day. Although I do find it strange that you're going to Montgomery Ink and not having a family member tattoo you. I thought that was sort of a *thing*."

I shrugged, and then set the towel down on the front seat. I ignored Kane's wince as I got onto his beautiful leather seats. Well, now his whole cabin was going to smell like shit, and I didn't care since that's what I smelled like.

"Hudson's good. And I've already had Leif and Sebastian ink me. Plus the uncles. I think I'm okay."

Our family was big. Okay, that was an understatement when it came to the Montgomerys.

Some of the Montgomerys had founded Montgomery Ink in downtown Denver years ago, before I'd even been born. Then they'd opened a second shop in Colorado Springs with a few of my aunts and uncles. And then a couple of my cousins had decided to open the next generation and call it Montgomery Ink Legacy. It happened to be right next door to our shop. The Montgomery family itself owned the building, and we therefore owned the four offices within it. With Montgomery Security, Montgomery Legacy, a cafe and coffee shop, and an art studio and gallery. I didn't much go to the latter, but some of my cousins ran it, so it was all in the family.

My cousin Leif had done my first tattoo, and then

my Uncle Austin had done another. My Aunt Maya had scooted in and done my third, and then Sebastian had done one more. I had another aunt and uncle as well as countless friends who could tattoo more as I thought of new things to get, but Hudson was the new tattoo artist at Montgomery Ink.

The fact that he happened to be Claire's brother didn't make me a stalker.

No, I just wanted to ensure I got the best. And make sure that Hudson knew that we thought he was one of the best.

"He does great work, and I want to encourage him. If a Montgomery lets him do work, that means he's aces. Plus it's just the sketch today. It's going to be a big piece, so it'll take time. I'll get inked right after we get back from vacation."

"I see the rationalization. But are you just trying to tell Claire that you believe in her and her family?"

"Has she even answered Phoebe's calls?" I asked, ignoring his question with one of my own.

"Yes. And they go out to lunch, and she's even spent the night at our place when I was forced to sleep on the couch and watch movies myself. Apparently, it was girl time."

My lips twitched at that. "Really."

"Really. I could have gone to your place, but you were having the plumber issues."

I winced. "It's okay, I called the cousins, and they fixed it."

"You should just have them do the whole house. You didn't need to buy some shoddy work and do it yourself. You work as many hours as any of us, and you're not a certified contractor like our cousins. Not quite sure what you're thinking."

"I'm thinking that I just want to figure things out. I'm sorry. I want to do things myself. Have it be my hands that fix it."

"Like the hands that kept you steady on that ladder when Bosley knocked you off it?"

"Fuck you." Though I had to hold back a smile.

"No, thanks. You're the one that smells like dog shit. I'm going to go with a no on that."

"I hate you."

"Maybe." We pulled into the parking lot, and I was grateful for the employee lot because the place was busy. Between the tattoo shop, our clients, the art studio, and the cafe, people were constantly in and out. It was good for business, bad for parking.

"Claire's fine. She's talking to people. She's working. And she sees Phoebe. I don't know why she's not answering your calls but Phoebe's watching her and so am I. And so is Aria and all of the other girls. Maybe it's you."

"I hate the fact that you're probably right," I grumbled.

"I know you didn't do anything to her, but I don't know... Claire's still weird around me just a little."

I paused in the act of opening the door and glared at him. "What do you mean? You didn't mention that before."

He looked around the parking lot, as if expecting Claire to show up. Claire never showed up. That was the problem.

"We were the ones who were there. Phoebe's her best friend, practically her sister, so she'll open up to her. But us? We were the ones who entered the room when she was hurt. Both of us had ended up bleeding and needing a few stitches in the process—though not as many as her. It was traumatic. And I'm not a therapist, so I'm not going to dive any deeper into that."

The idea that Kane's thoughts aligned with my own felt like a punch in the gut. "I just don't want her to hate me."

"She doesn't hate you." He paused as he stared at me. "Shit, man. I didn't know you had *feelings* for her."

I nearly fell out of the truck, going for full grace today. "No. It's not like that. I just don't like people not liking me. You know?"

It was a flaw—one I knew very well. But I had

known my entire life. After all, I had not one, not two, but three loving parents. I was a product of one of the famous Montgomery Triads, and I had two brothers who I loved with every ounce of my being. We were close as hell, and in addition to them, people just liked me. I wanted to know what the hell I had done to Claire.

Only I didn't think there were going to be any answers. So we slid out of the truck, and I ignored the pointed looks from my team as I walked through the building and into the back showers. I would forever be grateful for the fact that my cousin Daisy had said we needed office showers. I had been a little confused why, but the number of times we had shown up with blood or dirt on us from random experiences, told me that maybe this job was a little weirder than some people might think. I showered and changed into another set of clothes, grateful that I seemed to have a whole closet here and made my way to the tattoo shop next door. I still had a couple more days of work before my forced vacation—so I could use up those days—and this was only the start of it.

Leif was in his front booth as I walked in, and he tilted his chin at me. "Hey, Hudson's in the back, you can go sit in his booth. I still can't believe that you're letting a non-Montgomery ink you."

"Cold man," Nick said, and raised his pierced brow at me.

I flipped both of them off and made my way to Hudson's booth. "I still haven't let Nick tattoo me. Maybe he's next."

"He's practically a Montgomery. But still, next has to be a Montgomery. If you're going to do this, you're going to have to alternate." Leif's eyes were twinkling as he said it, a smirk on his face, so I knew he was only kidding. We might be territorial but we weren't complete idiots.

Hudson walked in, tall, broad-shouldered, and brown hair pulled back into a stub of a ponytail. He flicked his tongue over his lip ring and raised a brow at us. "You see, I knew inking a Montgomery was going to start some form of feud. However, with so many of you out there, it's just sheer statistics I'm going to get at least one of you."

He winked at me, and I rolled my eyes. "I'm excited for you to work on my arm piece. You do fantastic gray scale."

"I do, don't I?" Hudson asked, a broad smile on his face.

Nick whistled through his teeth. "He's as cocky as a Montgomery."

"You're married to one, so watch it," Leif grumbled, before they turned on music, and Hudson sat down in front of me.

"I'm really excited for this. I'm excited to flesh out

the art concept you're thinking about since I know placement's going to be an issue. The fact that it's eventually going to connect to a larger piece by another artist is pretty intriguing to me." He frowned at me, gesturing to my wet hair. "You showered? Long day?"

"I don't really want to talk about it. But I'm all clean. Don't worry."

"I feel like I should worry. That seems a little awkward."

I laughed and then we sat to go over the designs and placement. Because I wanted the art to feel like it could move with the flow of my other work and how I moved my body, we had to work on stencils too. It was a longer process than some of my other work, but since this was my first time working with Hudson, we wanted to make sure we got it right.

I loved ink. I loved the art and the statements that it made. I loved the fact that it could be something ridiculous, or something that moved you.

My family was filled with artists in one way or another, and I was grateful they hired people with amazing talent as well. I liked the feel of needle on skin, as it was a familiar pain, and I would ease my way into it, knowing it wasn't the worst thing I ever felt.

After all, I had been shot before, and stabbed. But that was when we had been working with the company prior to building our own. We needed to be trained somewhere, and we had taken harder jobs. Of course, I'd also been blown up in a building along with my cousin Daisy, but we had survived. Barely.

And as if I had conjured moments of terror and memories in my mind, the door opened, and Claire walked in.

My mouth went dry, but I ignored that. Because she was real. And she was here. I hadn't seen her in months, and it was all I could do not to fall down in front of her and beg her to tell me why she was avoiding me.

But that would make me feel like a stalker, so I didn't say anything. Instead, I just watched as her chin lifted slightly, and her eyes darted around the room until they landed on Hudson. She had elf-like features—so tiny, almost like a pixie. She had cut her hair to below her shoulders, and it was this brownish color that the word brown really didn't give justice to. It almost had natural auburn highlights, and she was beautiful.

I had always thought so. Even when I told myself I shouldn't.

But she was Phoebe's friend. And she had clearly wanted nothing to do with me. And her brother currently had a marker and stencil against my skin. So I wasn't going to think anything about that.

"Hey there, Claire Bear."

Claire's gaze shot to mine even though it was her brother who spoke, and she froze, her face paling, and I hated myself more than anything.

Because she looked scared to see me.

What the hell had I done?

Or rather, what the hell had I not done?

She dragged her gaze to her brother, ignoring me. "Oh, I have your dinner. Just wanted to stop by and drop it off before I go to my thing. I know you're busy. So I'll head out."

"You can come over," Hudson said, confusion etched on his face. "You know everybody here."

"I'm going to be late. But I'll just leave it here on the counter. Love you." She darted out, and Hudson frowned again.

"What the hell was that about?" he asked.

"No clue." It was all I could do not to ask Hudson if she was okay. Because she clearly wasn't. But I wasn't going to get anything from him. Instead Hudson frowned harder, and then he went back to work, and I let the sound of the needle and the motor from surrounding artists filter out my thoughts.

By the time we were settled into what we wanted, I smiled at the other man in the mirror's reflection. "It's going to look amazing."

"It already does," Hudson said with that cocky air, and I grinned.

We settled on a time for the next appointment, and I showed my cousins the work as they whistled through their teeth and congratulated Hudson on a job well done. I waved off invitations for dinner, just wanting to get home and be alone.

It had been a weird day, and I hadn't liked the look on Claire's face.

I just wanted to forget, and to be alone.

"Kingston?"

I froze, wondering why I wasn't keeping my attention on my surroundings better, when I looked up and saw Eddie, my friend from school who happened to live in my new neighborhood.

"Hey there. What are you guys doing here?" I asked, as I waved at him and his wife Samantha.

I had known Eddie back in elementary school, and then he had moved away in middle school before moving back in high school. We had both gone to the same university here in Colorado, and now lived in the same neighborhood. It was weird that no matter how large the world could be, how many times you could move around, sometimes you gravitated toward others. And Eddie was always one of those people.

"Actually, we were looking for you," Samantha said, and from the way that her eyes darted around, I frowned.

"What's wrong?"

"Nothing's wrong," Eddie said, before he sighed as Samantha gripped his hip. "I really don't know how to begin this. And I didn't want to put it in a text."

On alert now, my gaze darted around the fully lit parking lot, and I moved closer. "Do you need my team?"

Eddie's eyes widened, and Samantha let out a laugh. It was one of those laughs that seemed to have surprised her, as if she hadn't done it often recently. "No nothing like that. We're safe. Well. Hell."

Eddie ran his hands over his face, as his wife held him close. "I wasn't really planning on saying this in the middle of a parking lot in front of your place of business. We could have stopped by your house, but well, we're kind of running out of time. And then we were here, and I thought maybe I'd ask you for a cup of coffee and blurt everything out."

Eddie rarely rambled and this worried me. "What's going on, Eddie?"

"The cancer's back," Eddie blurted, his face crumbling, as Samantha's remained stoic—ever the strength in the face of horror.

I stood there, that odd buzzing sound in the back of my head going louder and intensifying over time until it was a sharp pinching. The pain from the tattoo was gone, all confusion from my day whispered away in that instance.

We'd been in college the first time Eddie had cancer. The first time I'd stared death in the face and realized there was nothing I could do except pray and hoped to hell that science and doctors could do their work. I'd been a bone marrow match for Eddie. Out of all of his family, he'd only had one match in his life—me. His friend. I'd donated as early as I'd been able, going through the entire process while waiting on pins and needles to see the results. And now I knew exactly what to say—even if I didn't know if these were the right answers.

"I'm so fucking sorry. When do you need me? Anything you want, Eddie. I'm here."

And when his wife broke down into my arms, Eddie wrapping his arms around her, I knew it was the right decision.

I couldn't fix most things. Hell, even today it felt as if I couldn't fix anything—not my job, not Claire, and not whatever I was feeling in that instant.

But maybe, just maybe, I could fix this.

2

CLAIRE

"I cannot tell you how much I love this, Claire. You literally took a simple idea that I had offhand and made it the best birthday party I have ever had in my life."

I smiled at my client's words, knowing they were only slightly slurred. It had been an amazing party after all, including a champagne bar with different sugar cubes and fruit to put in the champagne. And no matter how much water I also shoved down the throats of these guests, they'd indulged a little too much. But that was their prerogative. Because I had also planned rides for everyone. There would be no drunk driving on my watch.

"I'm just happy you're happy. Now go enjoy yourself. We've got it from here."

She hugged me tightly, having done it so quickly I hadn't been able to brace myself. I stiffened for just a bare instant, as if bracing for the blow. I didn't think Jasmine noticed though. Instead she just hugged me again, giggling in my ear, before skipping off with her friends to go enjoy her thirtieth birthday.

I swallowed hard, then ran my hands down my dove-gray slacks and told myself to get a reality check. Everything was fine. Nobody was out to get me. Nobody was going to hurt me.

"Claire?"

I turned to Trix and grinned, though I knew it probably didn't reach my eyes. "What can I do for you, Trix?""

"You were just standing there for a second. Are you okay?"

I held back a wince at her words, because I knew she was just worried about me. Like everybody was worried about me. It had been six months since the attack.

It had been six months since the feeling of ice-cold steel burned through my flesh and dug around on my insides. I knew that it wasn't ice-cold, and it wasn't an actual fiery hot poker. But every memory I had was of the two.

I had tried to protect my friend, and tried to get us out of a terrible situation that so many people were doing their best to protect us from, and I had failed. But

I was *fine*. I no longer had phantom pain. The scar would one day be a memory. And when enough time passed, my brother would tattoo over it, and I would never have to look at it again.

So why did I flinch when someone hugged me?

"Claire?"

I shook my head, knowing that it was probably scaring my team members. The fact that I even had people that I hired to help with events and parties was insane to me.

Trix was my right-hand woman, well, and my left-hand. She was the only person I hired with a regular paycheck, while everyone else was hired per-diem based on what I needed for any given event. It was all I could do for now, but one day it would be more. At least I hoped so.

"Sorry. Off in my own world. Long hours." Not quite a lie.

"That's why I was over here. You should go home. We'll handle all the cleaning and everything. You've handled all the admin, and we'll double-check that all the drivers know their positions and assignments, and we have it all. You should go home. Go see Phoebe. I know you said you would try to see her if you got out of here on time. So let's make that happen."

"You don't have to do that. I like being here."

Trix gave me that perfected look of hers. At the

moment, she had bubblegum pink hair in a lovely coiffed to-do up top with the sides shaved. The gem on her nose ring matched the color of her hair, and she had on a white suit without a speck of dirt on it. I wasn't quite sure how she had accomplished that considering the woman had been crawling on the ground looking for a diamond ring lost by one of the guests earlier. She had found it and hadn't ended up with a single stain. It was like magic.

But right then though, she gave me the expression of someone who was sick of my bullshit. Frankly, I was sick of my bullshit too, but it wasn't like I knew what I was supposed to say in this moment. *I'm sorry for flaking out, and for worrying everyone. I'm sorry that you and my brother and all of my friends and even people I didn't know were my friends were so worried about me that they seemed to have created a phone tree just to check on me.* No, I didn't think I was supposed to say any of that. But I wasn't quite sure there were words.

"Go home. You've already worked a twelve-hour day, and the birthday girl has already thanked you, and has seen you around every single instant she has needed you. I can handle this, and so can the team you have trained. You're doing great."

"But what if someone needs something..."

"Then let *us* handle it. You trained us well, boss."

"I know you guys can handle it. That's not the problem. But what if they want to set up a meet for another event?"

That was the big thing with my business. Word of mouth literally kept my business afloat or killed it.

"You have given your information to six people so far, and I have it right here." She tapped the little fanny pack on her side that blended in with her suit. It was still stain-free. Still not quite sure how she made that happen.

"But—"

Trix held up her hand and gave me an oh-so-patient look. "I love you with all of my heart. Now go home. To that beautiful home that you just bought and rarely stay in. You deserve it. You're a homeowner."

"I know I'm a homeowner. It still feels weird."

I had been an apartment renter for longer than I had planned. But I had loved living with Phoebe, and we both owned our own businesses, which meant there wasn't always enough money for things like a mortgage. But the perfect little cottage had fallen into my lap—probably thanks to the Montgomerys—and I couldn't walk away from it.

So now I was a homeowner of a home I rarely stayed in.

Because I lived there alone.

And I didn't want to live alone all the time.

However, I pushed those thoughts from my mind,

and knew that Trix was right because the longer I let myself stand here while she stared at me, worried for me, the more she would worry.

And there were only so many times I could lie to everyone's faces and tell them that I was fine when I clearly wasn't.

"You know what, you're right. I'm going to go home, heat up one of the many leftover meals I have in the freezer, and put my feet up."

"You know what? I believe some of that, but I have a feeling you'll only put your feet up so you can put your laptop on your lap and actually get some work done."

"Potato Potato," I said, saying the words with the same pronunciation, as she rolled her eyes at me, and I left her to do a quick look around before being forcibly pushed into my car by two of the team members. They did it with laughter in their eyes and didn't actually touch me for which I was grateful, but I knew when I had lost all ability to make my own choices.

I was defeated and had to get work done.

Darn it.

I was an event planner. I not only planned birthday parties like this extravagant affair that I put nearly too many working hours in to execute, I planned weddings, retirement parties, anniversaries, reunions, and just parties for the sake of parties. In a world where sometimes there didn't seem to be any light, or where we forgot to celebrate the little wins because the goalpost of the big wins kept moving further and further, my job was to celebrate those moments. Yes, I was a party planner, but I wasn't all Party City with fake pointy hats and balloons. I strived to be elegant, or down-home, ideally with whatever budget somebody needed.

I had a business degree, and countless contacts. One of my friends from college had gone straight into wedding planning, and only did that. And you could have a fulfilling and very full career in my business doing just that. But as someone who had maintained a crush for far too long without any reciprocated feelings, looking into happy ever afters every day probably wasn't good for my health. So I planned all parties.

Including divorce parties, funerals, and breakup girl-time parties.

Those weren't celebrations in some cases—no, those were moments in time when you needed your circle to remind you that you were okay.

I pulled into my driveway and looked at the small cottage that was just mine and smiled. It was my home. Just mine. And nobody could take that away from me.

A shiver slid down my back, but I ignored it. Nobody was watching me; nobody cared what I was doing. Nobody noticed me. And that was all for the best. I wasn't the one in trouble, nor was I the one in pain anymore.

Just as I was closing the garage door, still inside my car, I noticed headlights. My pulse raced, and I gripped my steering wheel, that flight response hitting hard, until I realized who was behind the wheel. Phoebe waved before the garage closed fully, and I realized that Trix must have called her.

Because of course she would have.

I wasn't sure I would have even contacted Phoebe at all without her reaching out first.

What kind of friend did that make me?

I let out a breath and knew that tonight would be good for me, even if I wasn't quite sure I believed it myself. As soon as I got inside, there was a knock at the door, and I went to it, and undid the two deadbolts and the safety chain. You could never be too safe. I also tapped the security panel that Kane and the Montgomerys had installed at the cottage for me. They were the top firms in the business, and I had done my best not to feel poorly for running away and looking busy with work when Kane had been in the house to help set it up.

He was always checking on me like I was his kid sister. Even though I had never thought of him in a brotherly way. No...it was another Montgomery that plagued my mind for *far* different reasons.

I opened the door, and it wasn't just Phoebe there, but Aria as well.

A true smile slid over my face, and I stepped back as they walked inside. I quickly closed the door behind them, locking it quickly and setting the alarm again. I tried to be as casual as possible, but I knew they saw. They always did.

But they didn't say anything or give each other sly looks. After all, Aria had worked with Montgomery Security before she had moved to work on her true passion, and Phoebe had been in the same room as I had, both of us screaming for help. I knew she and Kane had just as many locks.

"So let me guess, either you've tracked me with some form of GPS I'm unaware that I have on my person, or Trix called you?"

"Why can't it be both?" Aria asked, as she held up two bags of takeout. "We brought Indian food as well. That way you can save your leftovers for another night."

I smiled, and kissed Aria's cheek. "I like my leftovers, but I like takeout Indian food more."

"Same," Phoebe said before she kissed my cheek, and we headed to the kitchen.

"I'm glad you're both here," I said, realizing that it was true.

"Where else would we be?" Aria asked.

There was something in my friend's tone that I couldn't quite catch, but then she just smiled at me, and I realized maybe I was the one trying to see things that weren't there.

"Okay, so how was the birthday party?" Phoebe asked, as she made herself at home in my kitchen and pulled out plates. I smiled at the thought and went to her side to pull out glasses. Phoebe and I had been roommates in college, and afterward. It was odd to think that she wasn't either across the living room in common areas, or not in the room next door. In fact, she lived a good ten minutes away, thanks to traffic. I couldn't just blink and she would be at my side anymore. I hated it, but I loved the fact she was so happy. She deserved it. Especially with everything that had happened with her family recently.

"It went really well. I'm surprised Trix didn't tell you." I said the last part a little sarcastically, and Aria snorted.

"Don't be mad at her. I'm glad she called Phoebe. And I happened to be there annoying her." Aria winced. "I know I wasn't technically invited, but I'm here. So you have to deal with me too."

"And I'm grateful you're here," I said, meaning it.

"And I wasn't invited either. But we're here. And she's just going to have to get over it. So, how's life?" Phoebe asked as we plated up our dinner.

"Normal. Just busy. Tons of work, and I'm still trying to figure out paint colors."

I looked around the taupe-colored room but didn't wince. It wasn't exactly my shade, nor was the house decorated or upgraded the way I wanted. I planned to keep the cottage feel, but upgrade some of the appliances when I had money. I also wanted to finish unpacking, something I hadn't done, but they didn't need to look into my spare room. No, I didn't even want to look in there.

"So really, what happened at the birthday party? Did she have a huge cake or go the cupcake route?" Aria asked. "I don't really care about the difference between cakes or cupcakes, other than I want both. We really should have stopped at a bakery."

"I made some cookies last night when I was thinking. Red velvet with cream cheese frosting."

"I love you," Aria raptured, as she bit into her chicken korma.

Phoebe winked at me. "And that's why I didn't pick up dessert, because you always have some baked good here when you're stressed or trying to think. I've missed them so much since we moved."

I smiled, ignoring the little pain at the fact we were no longer roommates. "I'll make sure you have some to take home. I still bake for forty. But the party was nice. I might want to do something like that for my thirtieth."

"You have a couple of years until that happens," Phoebe teased.

"I don't know, I like birthday parties. I just like parties."

Aria laughed. "Well, it's good that you're a party planner then."

"I actually almost called you," I said, pointing my fork at her.

"Oh?" Aria asked.

"My photographer almost flaked, but she showed up at the last moment. And I realize that you're not an event photographer, and purposely not a wedding photographer, but I was desperate and was about to have to use my phone."

Aria shuddered. "No, I'm not an event photographer, but I would help you out in an instant if you needed it. Please don't use your phone. I've got you."

"That's good to know. But I don't want to have to rely on my friends for every emergency."

"We don't mind," Phoebe said, as she squeezed my arm, before giving herself a whole body shake. "I had to fire a client today," Phoebe muttered. "So I'm glad you had a good day."

"What happened?" I asked, an odd sense of alarm slamming into me. And I had no idea where it came from. Or rather, I did, and I didn't want to worry about it.

"Oh, just late payments and being an absolute mess. And then they wanted to practically steal a design from another designer, and I didn't want anything to do with it. So I fired them, but thankfully I have a backup plan for this month's income. It's just a pain in the ass."

"I'm sorry," I said.

Aria nodded. "People suck. But we're here and we don't suck."

"That's really what we should put on our matching T-shirts. Of course, we'll have to change Phoebe's up a bit because I know Kane wouldn't appreciate it." I blinked innocently as I said it, and Phoebe choked on her water, as Aria kicked her feet and laughed.

"I cannot believe you just said that," Phoebe teased, and I did my best not to meet her eyes, before I dug into my meal, and we continued to talk about our days, our lives, and I tried not to double-check the locks, or the camera feed. Nobody needed to worry that we were safe or not. Because everything was locked up tight. And I would triple-check before bed after the girls left. Everything was fine.

I was completely safe.

So why did I feel as if that were a complete lie?

3

KINGSTON

It's funny how time can move in a blink of an eye or drag on in its infinite existence as if it took every ounce of your life along the way.

That's how I felt as I sat in the doctor's office, for yet another consultation, going over everything that needed to happen.

Once Eddie and Samantha had dried their tears and sucked in breaths, we had gone into Latte on the Rocks, the café in our building. We had sat down so that way they could get some tea, and frankly I just needed the coffee. It probably wasn't the best idea to have caffeine when I was still on a high from a tattoo, and the crash of what had just happened, but we needed to sit and talk.

And then plans had been made.

I had donated bone marrow before, so I remembered the initial pain, and all the discussions—but it had been a while.

Even though we had already done all the testing before to ensure it was a perfect match, we did it again. And so between blood tests and a physical exam, I was finally ready.

And now it was a couple of weeks later and I sat in a hospital room, my hands on my knees since I still wore my normal clothes and hadn't yet been put into a gown.

Samantha and Eddie were in another part of the hospital and thankfully they wouldn't be in the same room as me for this. No, somebody would just be using a very large fucking needle to withdraw liquid marrow from both sides of the back of my pelvic bone. It didn't matter that eventually I would be given anesthesia, and I wouldn't feel any pain during the donation. I would still know that there was a needle scraping inside of me and digging out liquid marrow.

Honestly, for a man who had tattoos, I was still afraid of needles. At least large ones that went down to the bone that is. In a world where my friends routinely got hurt or were sick, I felt as if maybe a slight fear of needles wasn't such a terrible thing to be worried about.

And so now I sat on the edge of the hospital bed, as my mother looked through my bag ensuring I had everything in case I needed to stay overnight. The doctor didn't think I would and felt I would be able to go home that evening and sleep in my own bed—however uncomfortable—but it didn't matter to my mother. Because sometimes you had to stay overnight, so she wanted to make sure I had everything. I was an adult, but Holland Montgomery always made sure that her kids were well taken care of.

She had pulled her hair back from her face with two little clips on the side, and the curls just made her look far younger than she was. Of course, my mom had always just been Mom to me. Just like my dad Ethan, and my other dad Lincoln, were just Dad.

I hadn't grown up in the most conventional of homes and yet to some, it was beyond such. And although my childhood hadn't been the same as many others, I had been loved, cared for, and felt as if nothing had really been different than most of my friends.

While some people only had two parents, or one, or were parents of divorce and had two separate families, I happened to have two dads and one mom. My cousins Sebastian, Aria, Gus, and Dara all had the same situation with Aunt Maya and her two husbands. My dad just happened to be the Montgomery, and my brothers Logan and Oliver and I had three parents. It worked for us. Of course, that did mean I had an additional human being to hover over me like my dad Lincoln was doing right now.

"You had a bad reaction last time you were under anesthesia, so are you sure they're going to let you go home today?" he asked, and I sighed, running my hands over my face.

I only needed one person with me because someone had to drive me home. I didn't want both of my brothers and all three of my parents, nor my cousins hanging around. But of course, Kane and Phoebe were in the waiting room along with Logan and Oliver, while all three of my parents were in the room with me, hovering.

I didn't have time to be nervous or worried about what would happen or even if this would work because damn it, this had to work.

All I could do was try to reassure them which helped me in the long run. Who knew?

I just had to make sure they understood I would be fine, and everything would work out in the end, and reassure them that I wasn't stressed out over what was about to happen.

And I knew that they were somewhat doing this on purpose because my three parents were the most self-assured and confident people I knew. After all, living in an open poly relationship where not only did my dads love my mom, but they also loved each other? That wasn't for the weak of heart. They had survived the worst, been through terror, and I was so damn grateful they were my parents.

Only I really wanted to get this day over with.

"I've been under anesthesia more than once because of my job and was fine then," I countered.

"I don't think mentioning the whole being blown up and stabbed and shot at thing is really going to help us now," my other dad Ethan said, as he studied some of the photos on the wall. "Why do they show so many blood vessels and random things on the walls? Shouldn't they show you something a little more soothing before any kind of procedure?"

"I'm sure they'll have a soothing landscape water-color for him later," my mom said dryly. "I'm pretty sure they only put these up so people can learn a few things since our education system is seriously lacking."

I pressed my lips together, holding back a smile. "You do realize that I'm a grown man and don't need all three of you in here hovering?" My parents merely glared at me, and I held up both hands. "You know what, that's fine. Everything is going to be fine."

Lincoln pulled up his phone again. "Okay, common side effects of marrow donation are around two days in and it's back and hip pain, fatigue, even throat pain, muscle pain, insomnia."

"Don't forget headaches, dizzy, and loss of appetite," Ethan added.

"Some people can recover in two days or a week, other times it can take a whole month or a year," Mom put in.

"Did you guys memorize that one website?" I asked.

"We looked at *multiple* websites," my mom said, before she moved forward and cupped my cheeks. "It scared me so much when you were sick the first time, but you were going to help your friend, and I love you with all of my heart. You care about so many people, my Kingston. And I'm honored to be your mother." She leaned forward and kissed the tip of my nose.

I swallowed the lump in my throat and reached up to grip her wrists and squeezed. "I'll be okay. Eddie needs me."

"I know, baby. I know."

"We all tested to see if we were a match the first time," Ethan said as he cleared his throat. "And we would all do this, but you're doing it for a second time. And I so love you for it."

"I'll be okay, you guys," I whispered, and she then she kissed my forehead, and let me go before each of my dads hugged me tight.

As soon as they moved back, the nurses came in, and then it was time to prepare.

The procedure was very similar to the first, with no

pain, just an uncomfortable sensation. And this time I didn't react to the anesthesia adversely, so I was able to go home after they checked my vitals, and they waited for any reaction.

I wouldn't hear from Samantha or Eddie for a bit, and that was fine. We needed to make sure that Eddie's body didn't reject the donation, and everything was grafted the way that it should.

It had worked before, and it would again.

And while I knew that having already donated twice in my life was a rarity, if I somehow matched again to someone else, or if Eddie needed a third, I would do it. Although I knew I probably needed to recover.

They could take what they needed, just to keep him safe.

I was strong enough—I had to be.

BY THE TIME I got home, the family hadn't left me alone.

Instead, the parents were cooking in the kitchen, making sure that I had plenty of things to heat up. The fact that they had made sure that the pans they put in the freezer weren't too heavy so I wouldn't have to lift anything was ridiculous, but caring.

They understood me. And they were damn good at it.

"So your ass hurt?" Oliver, my youngest brother, asked. It didn't matter that we were all in our twenties and I was approaching thirty, Oliver was still my baby brother.

Emphasis on *baby*.

"Really? That's where you're going with this?"

"I know, it's all about your hips. Wasn't there that old song about your hips not lying or something?" he asked.

"I cannot believe you just called it an old song," Mom called from the kitchen, and I held back a chuckle. Laughing too hard didn't feel quite great.

While everything was still numb, and I didn't have too much discomfort, it was going to hit me soon. I was tired, and while I liked having my family here— including Kane and Phoebe here—I really just wanted some peace and quiet.

"You guys don't need to stay all day. I promise I'm okay."

"One of us is going to stay with you all night. Just in case. We're here for you, and you're just going to have to deal with it," Mom said firmly. I smiled and settled deeper into the couch.

I lay back and watched my family eat as the nausea had hit me, and I wasn't sure if it was from the anesthesia, or the donation itself. So I did my best to get comfortable with some saltines and ginger ale.

Kane and Phoebe—who had arrived for dinner—left first, and I knew they did because they wanted to set the tone, and then my parents finally left, leaving just my brothers.

When they flipped a coin, I wasn't quite sure if it was who wanted to stay with me, or who wanted to leave, but then Oliver was the only one left, and he pulled out his book and settled in the chair in front of the TV.

"Are you just going to read all night in the chair in your clothes and not do anything else?"

"I figured I'd go take your bed later and sleep since you're going to be out here."

"You're so giving," I said dryly, while Oliver winked in reply. We looked just alike, dark hair, blue eyes, with that strong jaw that came from both of my fathers.

At the moment Oliver was still in school, and I knew he was figuring out what he wanted to do with the rest of his life. He was completing his gen eds, and finding his path, and that's what I liked about our family. There was no pressure to figure out what you wanted to be when you grew up, when you were only sixteen or seventeen. You had time to make it work. The fact that Oliver could ace all of his exams and his gen eds meant that he had many paths he could choose. He just needed to do it. And we Montgomerys would be his net in case he wanted to fly and didn't make it the first round.

I had gotten lucky by finding what I wanted. I had thought about joining the military, maybe even trying for the Air Force Academy, but in the end, I had gone for business, with a few other specialties. We had worked for other security companies, ones that had ended up not being a great fit for us. Mostly because a few of the guys had been former mercenaries, and that hadn't been the path we wanted. Our Uncle Border had built a company from scratch, and so we had relied on him to help determine our paths, and I would be forever grateful we were never alone in any of this.

I loved my job, even the danger that came with it. I liked the adrenaline.

I just hated failing.

There was a soft rap at the door, and I rolled my eyes.

"Will you make sure that whichever family member is there knows that I'm fine and I'll see them tomorrow?"

Oliver grunted and went to answer the door. I didn't even bother looking at the camera considering I had some of the best security out there. Oliver would deal with it and had already looked at the screen.

When he winked over his shoulder at me, I was

confused as to who it could be on the other side of that door. "Well, hello there," Oliver said, as he drawled out the words, and leaned against the doorway. He did that pose we had all seen once in a movie, and I knew for a fact that Oliver practiced in the mirror.

Who the hell was on the other side of that door?

"Oh, you're Logan, right?" a very familiar, very sultry voice asked, and I sat up too quickly, letting out a harsh groan.

The pain came out of nowhere because I was an idiot for moving like I had, so I couldn't even relish the fact that she had gotten the wrong brother's name.

"I'm actually Oliver. Come on in."

"Oh, I just wanted to drop this off."

"No, you should totally come in," he said. And as the stars finally faded from my vision, I looked up to see Claire standing there, a tin container in hand, and worry on her face.

She was so fucking beautiful.

And that was something I needed to stop thinking.

"Are you in pain? Oh my God, are you hurting?" she asked, and I shook my head.

"No, I just sat up too fast. I'm glad my brother let you in."

"Well, since I see you're in good hands, I'm going to head over to the bedroom. You know, just to read or something. Have a good night." And then Oliver grabbed his book and ran away.

Very subtle, my little brother.

"Hi," Claire said, and I swallowed hard again.

"Hi."

I just stared at her face, those beautiful cheekbones, those long lashes, and I wasn't quite sure what I was supposed to say.

Claire was in my house. The person that had been avoiding me for weeks, months, was in my house.

And I was sitting here on the couch, with my ginger ale and crackers, not feeling like the normal guy I should be.

"Thanks for coming. I didn't even know you knew I'd been in the hospital." I paused, realizing she hadn't said anything about that. "Unless you're just here for something else?"

She shook her head, then held out the tin awkwardly. "I'm here with cookies. A peace offering."

I frowned again, trying to keep up. I was still a little off, it seemed. "A peace offering for what, Claire?"

Her face fell, as did her arms. So she set the tin down on the coffee table and let out a deep breath. "I've been really off since the attack. I've been mean to you. And I don't know why. Well, I sort of do, but that's fine. I heard what you did, and I just want to say that's amazing. *You're* pretty amazing."

I shook my head, uncomfortable for a completely different reason now. "Anyone would do it. I'm not amazing for doing the right thing."

She moved forward then, a frown etched on our features. I didn't like seeing her frown. I wanted to make her smile.

"It's more than that. Not everyone does something so unselfish, not everyone can. You are trying to save someone's life, something you do all the time, and you don't even realize it. So I'm just here to say I'm sorry. I should have been here before...before you donated bone marrow and saved someone with cancer. I should have said thank you for helping me that day, and I'm sorry that I've been out of it. I'm trying to get back to being myself. I'm trying to be better. So I just wanted to come here and let you know that I won't be mean anymore. And I won't ignore your calls."

I really felt like I was missing something here, but I wasn't sure what I was supposed to say. "Just like that. You won't tell me why?" I asked.

"Just know it's really me. It's not you." She winced. "I know that's trite."

"I'm not even sure I know what trite means," I said with a laugh.

She smiled then, and it felt as if I had once again won the lottery. Or maybe just finally won something. "Are you really okay though? Does it hurt?"

"It's going to in a bit. I'm still a little dozed out from the anesthesia. And they did a nerve blocking thing, I think? I'm not really making up good words right now."

"Do you want me to go?"

"Stay," I blurted, not even realizing I was saying it until the word was already out.

"You want me to stay? Isn't your brother here? Or is someone supposed to be in the room with you the whole night?"

"No, I can take care of myself, I just want you to... stay. Let's watch a movie. Do something. And not talk about bone marrow or the fact that I just want these saltines and ginger ale."

She studied my face then, and I had to wonder what she was going to say, what she *could* say in that moment. But she set down her bag and finally sat down on the couch.

She was close to me, but it didn't feel close enough, so since I was just sitting there, I rearranged myself so that way I was leaning against the back of the couch, close enough to her.

And without any words, because I wasn't sure there were any words to say, we turned on a movie—I wasn't even quite sure what was happening on the screen—and I was able to eat a cookie. And as I fell asleep on the couch, with my head on her shoulder, I finally relaxed for the first time in far too long.

And it felt good.

And later, when I was in that half-dozed sleep and the movie was over, it felt as if her hands were in my hair.

But that couldn't be right. And that wasn't her whispering goodnight.

Instead, I just fell asleep, feeling content, as if I could save the world, and do anything.

Because Claire had come to me.

Finally.

Only I hadn't realized I had been waiting all this time.

4

CLAIRE

In the two weeks since I'd realized that I needed to heal the rift I'd caused between the man I'd had a crush on and myself, I hadn't really seen him. He'd been healing and then gone back to work on desk duty, and I'd been working overtime making sure that everything was set for me to take a week off for this trip.

I still couldn't believe I was going on a hiking trip in the Rocky Mountains in the middle of winter in Colorado with the Montgomerys, but once my friends began asking, it was hard to say no.

Honestly, it was always hard to say no to a Montgomery.

Including when they asked you to stay for a movie and not talk because they'd fallen asleep, and you couldn't help but watch them because you were so damn scared.

Because you were *always* so damn scared.

But that didn't matter in the moment. It couldn't.

"I'm so sorry that you have to drive up alone," Phoebe's voice rang out over the car speaker, as I kept both hands on the wheel, and meandered my way up the winding road into the mountains. Thankfully it wasn't snowing at the moment, but it had snowed the night before. Just a dusting to make it look picturesque, but a winter party with friends and the Montgomery family in the mountains was probably going to lead to only bad things. Mostly because for some reason my friends tended to end up in the hospital more often than not. Yes, I had joined them this last time, but I wasn't alone in that.

"You had a meeting that you couldn't cancel. It's after the holiday season, at least."

"Meaning I'm *still* doing decorations for events, beyond designing homes. You however, Ms. Party Planner. I cannot believe that you were able to take time off during your busiest season."

I winced at her comment but knew that me working hours upon hours to actually make this happen was for a reason.

"I'm allowed to take a couple of days off."

"You brought your computer with you, didn't you?"

"Of course I did. And I've been on work calls when I haven't been on the phone with you. Totally paying attention to the road and I'm not going to drive off into a ditch down a cliff."

"Okay, Claire. I'm hanging up. I want you to be safe."

"I'm okay. I promise." Out of the corner of my eye I saw a couple of deer or elk or some other horned creatures make their way through their own little path in the forest, and I prayed they wouldn't go in front of my car. Okay, maybe I needed to be paying better attention. But if I was talking about work or to my best friend, I wasn't worried about the fact that I would be spending a couple of days with Kingston and all of his friends and family.

"Hey, I have to go, babe. I have another meeting. But we'll be up a couple hours after you. I promise."

"I'll hold you to it. We'll get it all settled for you."

"I'm excited to see everybody. And just relax. A fun little Montgomery friend winter party in the woods. What could go wrong?"

"You realize I'm driving with snow around? Why would you even ask that? The Montgomerys pretty much have their name engraved in the hospital walls."

"I'll have you know we *are* in a few hospitals," Kane interjected. "We spread the wealth through the city of Denver. We're not just in one suburb."

I laughed along with them and as I said my good-byes, I tightened my hands on the steering wheel and made my way up the winding path.

The Montgomerys had owned a few cabins over the years within the family. Mostly because there were so many of them. They went in on them as a family and used them sort of as timeshares for just family members. The building was rarely empty, and now it was going to be home to ten of us tonight and the next night.

I still couldn't quite believe I was invited, but I was trying to do better. To be with my people.

And not shut myself off in my room all the time.

It just seemed easier to do that though.

I was honestly still nervous though because Kingston was going to be one of the people. Thankfully though, with the majority of them being Montgomerys, it wasn't completely coupled off. Aria I knew was bringing her friend, and Daisy and Hugh were also bringing their friend Crew, who happened to be good friends with another Montgomery, Lexington. So in the end, there were ten of us, but it wasn't all couples. The cabin was big enough for everybody to bunk together in pairs, but not so much that it would feel awkward. Aria and I were bunkmates, and there were two queen beds waiting for us.

And Kingston was going to be there. And I hadn't

even spoken to him since the night I went over to his house.

I had been working on stepping out of my comfort zone. About getting out of my house, about speaking to people. When I had heard that he had gone in for a painful and life-changing procedure for someone else, I hadn't been able to stay away.

And then I stayed there.

For hours.

It wasn't until Oliver had come out from the bedroom, looking sleepy-eyed, that I finally got up and tucked Kingston in on the couch. Oliver hadn't said anything, though I knew he had questions in his eyes.

I didn't have answers for anyone.

Instead I had gone home and hadn't spoken to Kingston since.

Only when he had texted me and thanking me for staying the night and for the cookies, I had given it a heart emoji, instead of a thumbs up emoji, or instead of ignoring him.

It was progress.

Somewhat.

I pulled up to the cabin, expecting to be one of the first people there. Mostly because I was early to everything. I knew Daisy and Hugh were going to be a little bit later because they had to drop off their daughter at her grandparents, but everyone else should've been arriving around the same time I was. Kane and Phoebe would be the latest ones because of Phoebe's meeting.

I got out of the car and inhaled the sweet mountain air. It was so crisp, clean, and it felt as if my entire world had shifted.

I was alone in this moment and the vastness of this earth, surrounded by mountains and tall trees, with the snow from earlier still on the ends of the branches slowly falling down onto the patches beneath.

It was going to snow again later today, but not too much. Just enough so we would have a little bit of a photo-op and be able to have the fire going full blast, and then we would sleep, eat, and just enjoy ourselves.

I had pulled up next to Kingston's car, and in that moment realized that no one else was there.

Well then.

When Kingston opened the door and walked down the steps of the two-story log cabin, I swallowed hard, and tried not to stare at the way that his thighs filled out those jeans, or how he had pulled the sleeves of his heather gray Henley up over his forearms.

He had pushed his hair back from his face and had on a gold bracelet that I knew his mother had given him one year for Christmas. He didn't wear it often, but he sometimes did with a leather beaded bracelet, or his watch.

I hated the fact that I had noticed all of these little things about him.

That's what happened when you had a crush on a man who hadn't even realized you were alive.

I hadn't meant to feel this way toward him. Not now, and surely not when we had first met. Phoebe and Kane had been going strong, sweet at first, innocent, and I had met Kingston on that same mountain.

A bear had scared us all, or at least me and Phoebe, and the experience had gotten us all together, and we had laughed and became friends.

Phoebe and Kane had clicked, and I had gotten all warm and tingly inside when I looked at Kingston.

And he had seen me as the little friend, maybe even a little sister.

And hadn't that been demoralizing?

"Hey, you're here." He smiled, that half smile of his that popped out that dimple. He was too handsome for his own good.

I nearly tripped over my feet, just standing there. I had no idea how it happened, but he did that to me. It tugged up my scar slightly, and I winced, pressing my hand to the side. I was fully healed, but every once in a while, I got a twinge.

Kingston's eyes widened and he nearly ran to me. "Claire? Are you okay?"

Embarrassed, I let my hand drop and I nodded. "Oh,

I'm fine. Sometimes I just tug on my scar. But you know it's life. You have scars too. That we don't need to talk about." I knew I was just blurting words at this point, so I had to make a full sentence. "How are you feeling?"

He studied my face, as if searching for far more answers than I had to give, before he gave me a nod, as if he were reaffirming that I was fine.

Such a big brother attitude.

"I'm good. Thankfully the nausea went away that evening, and I'm going to say it was thanks to your cookies."

I rolled my eyes. "Yes, because the intake of sugar was probably good for you."

"You never know. But I'm doing fine. No soreness at all. Thank God."

"That's good."

He cleared his throat as I just stared at him and realized that I wasn't sure what we were supposed to say. We used to be good at speaking to one another, having full conversations and talking about our days. Even when I'd been hopelessly attracted to him and everything about him, we'd been able to talk.

Then the attack happened, and nothing made sense anymore. And I'd finally come to terms with the fact that I had fallen for Kingston Montgomery, and he was never going to fall for me. So figuring that out had taken enough out of me *that I had hidden.*

But I didn't want to hide anymore. Even if that meant knowing nothing would happen with him again ever.

"Anyway, we're just waiting to hear from the doctors how the bone marrow transplant went, but I feel good about it. And so does my friend. I just got off a phone call with him, and he's in bright spirits. Crossing all the things, you know?"

"Oh, I'm glad to hear that he's feeling better. Hopefully everything grafts on and he's out of the woods soon. You did such an amazing thing, Kingston."

He immediately shook his head and frowned. I wondered what that was about. "It's what anyone would have done."

"We both know that's not the case."

"Well, it's something that I've done. And I'd do it again. Although I know this second time isn't going to be a sure thing, because the first one wasn't. But I'm still in the registry. If they need me, I'm there."

I swallowed hard, telling myself I was not supposed to fall for this man *again*. "You know Phoebe and I added ourselves to the registry. Went through the whole process. I know it's a very minuscule chance that we'll ever match with someone, but we're there."

"That's...that's really cool, Claire."

I continued on as if I wasn't rambling in stress and anxiety—my two true best friends. "Before all this happened actually, I was thinking about looking into being a living donor. Or doing something. You know, just because there's so much pain out there in the world you might be able to fix something. And you know that firsthand. But after the attack when it nicked my spleen, I'm not a good candidate for many things like that anymore."

His face fell, and I could have kicked myself for even saying anything. "I'm sorry, Claire."

"There really isn't anything to be sorry about," I whispered before clearing my throat. "There's nothing we can do, but I give blood when I can, and you give bone marrow. It's what we can do."

"Yes, so many bodily fluids." He seemed to realize what he just said, and I burst out laughing, grateful that things sounded normal.

"Okay then. And on that note, I'm going to go get my things out of my car and go see which room is mine."

"I put sticky notes on the doors at Daisy's request." He rolled his eyes as he said it, as he came with me to the back of my car.

"That sounds like something she'd ask you to do. And I can handle it."

"You can let me lift things."

"Are you allowed to? You were here first, meaning you brought up most of the food, didn't you?"

"Some of it. Everyone else is bringing something."

"I brought wine."

"See, Daisy put that on your list."

We smiled at each other for so long that I realized we were just staring awkwardly. "Okay, you can help me lift things, but not everything."

"Aren't you the one who said your scar just hurt?"

"Fine, we'll go a tiny little poundage at a time. What do you say?"

"I think we can take tiny poundage." He frowned. "You know, I don't have anything else to say to that."

I burst out laughing and pushed at his shoulder, and he just shook his head, as we took everything out of the SUV, and locked the doors behind it just in case a bear somehow got out of hibernation and decided to get inside. They were curious after all.

"Is everyone else on their way up?"

"They should be," he said as he pulled out his phone.

"Nobody's texting me, but we're getting a few weather alerts."

Alarms spread up my spine. "I've been driving and didn't see anything. What's going on?"

"Just the snowstorm gaining speed. It was supposed to bypass us completely, but it might have shifted. Once they get up here, we'll be fine. We've got generators and we have enough food even if they don't bring anything.

But I hope they get up the mountain quickly before they close the pass."

"Oh hell. I didn't even think about that."

"It'll be fine. It's always going to be an issue when you take trips out here, but we've done it before. And the alerts aren't that bad."

His phone buzzed again, and I nearly jumped in my skin before his jaw went tense.

"What's wrong. Did they close the pass?"

"No... I mean maybe. No, it's just Eddie."

My heart raced. "Oh. Do you want privacy?"

He shook his head as he answered, putting the phone on speakerphone. I stood there, not knowing what to do with my hands, or anything else. "Hey," Kingston said, his face full of smiles, brightness, and not a lick of worry.

He was so damn good at that. Hiding his own worry to help others.

He had been like that with me, except once.

When he had looked at me in the mirror, and I had seen worry etched on his face. And that was when I knew I had to let him go. At least the thought of him.

"Hey there. We have good news," Eddie said, and when Kingston nearly staggered, I put my hand on the small of his back, keeping him steady. I hadn't meant to, hadn't even thought about it, but then the heat of him was against my skin, and I couldn't let go.

"Really?"

"Yeah, things seem to be looking up. You have no idea what you've done."

"It was nothing."

"It was something. I just, I don't have words. You keep giving, and I'm so damn grateful for you in my life."

"I'm so damn grateful too," Eddie's wife called from the other side of the phone, and though I couldn't see them, I saw the way that Kingston's shoulders relaxed, and his eyes went a bit glassy.

They spoke for a few minutes more, and I could see the adoration in that man's face.

When they hung up, Kingston just beamed at me. "He's still in the hospital, but he's doing better. Fuck, he's doing better."

He set the phone down, and before I knew what was happening, he was taking me by the hips, and spinning me around the kitchen. I put my arms on his shoulders, laughing with him, as we danced to music nobody could hear, and he just grinned.

"So. He's doing great. Everything's fine. Oh, thank God."

"I'm so happy for you."

Kingston hugged me tightly then, resting his chin on top of my head, as he let out a deep, relieved sigh, and I held him close, feeling his heart beat rapidly against my ear.

We stood there for a moment in silence, but awkwardness hadn't settled in. Instead it felt normal.

What the hell was wrong with me?

When his phone buzzed again, we broke apart quickly, and then my phone buzzed in my back pocket.

I pulled it out and looked at the mess of text messages in the group chat.

"Oh my God," I muttered.

"Fuck," Kingston snapped.

> **CREW:**
>
> Well, I'm in a car with Aria and Travis, and we're stuck at the pass.

> **ARIA:**
>
> It looks like we're going to be turned around soon. Are you guys up there?

> **KANE:**
>
> No we're still at home, Phoebe's on a call.

> **DAISY:**
>
> We're just now heading up the highway, it took a while to get Nora to settle down.

> **HUGH:**
>
> Does that mean we need to turn around?

CREW:

> They're waving us around, so I need to
> get off the phone.

ARIA:

> Is anybody up there yet?

I looked at Kingston, an odd sensation settling my stomach, as he sighed and began to type.

KINGSTON:

> Claire and I are up here. We've got
> enough food and alcohol to last the
> night, hopefully we can head back
> down in the morning. But it looks like
> we're stranded up here.

My phone buzzed, but this time it wasn't the group chat, and Kingston raised a brow, but instead went back to look at the group chat that was now buzzing along with more messages. People saying they were sorry, and figuring out when they were going to plan something else. Others making sure that we were safe and had enough supplies in case the storm got bad.

But I looked down at the text that was solely for me.

PHOEBE:

> Are you going to be okay alone
> with him?

Had she known? All this time, had my best friend known?

What an idiotic question.

Of course Phoebe knew.

Me:

> We'll be fine. We have provisions. And separate bedrooms.

I tacked that one on, grateful Kingston couldn't see me typing.

PHOEBE:

Well, you know what they say, you may have more than one bed, but you might get cold at night.

ME:

> I have blankets. I'll be warm enough.

PHOEBE:

Just be careful. And have fun.

I ignored the extra emojis that I wasn't even going to name, as I set the phone down.

"Well...this isn't how we planned this weekend." I wasn't sure what else I was supposed to say.

"Pretty much. But we have entertainment, food, lots of wine, and I brought the good bourbon."

I grinned. "Bourbon?"

"I'll make some old fashioneds. After we make sure the house is safe. Looks like it's going to be a long night."

And as he moved away to check whatever needed to be checked, I sighed.

Oh, a long night wasn't even going to be the half of it.

5

KINGSTON

T his wasn't exactly how I had planned to spend my evening, nor my vacation; however, in the end, it could have been worse. Snow began to accumulate on the windowsill and the trees as well as on top of our cars, but it wasn't too cold outside. Meaning we weren't going to end up with heavy ice on branches, or other issues that would mean power loss, or us having to deal with things we rather wouldn't.

So I was grateful for that at least.

And it was damn beautiful out, even with the wind and snow, and I didn't mind the view.

Of course, I wasn't exactly only looking outside the window.

I had a very strong old fashioned in my hand, and

Claire stood in the kitchen, bright smile on her face, as she added a whiskey cherry to hers.

"These are potent," she said, her hips moving to the music as she moved around the room.

I adjusted myself in my jeans, a little worried about the fact that I got so hard when she was around. That wasn't exactly what I had been planning on showcasing, but it wasn't as if I could change that. I couldn't control what my body did when it came to seeing her.

Then again, that happened often.

That first time we had seen each other in the forest, I had sucked in a sharp breath, and been enraptured by her face.

Yes, she had been a little fierce, a little manic since a bear had walked past the park restroom where she had been hiding, but she had been so full of energy, I couldn't help but laugh right along with her.

And then we saw the instant connection between Kane and Phoebe, and I had taken a step back.

Frankly, Claire was good as my friend. And I liked that.

I liked the fact that it was easy around her. Or at least, it had been.

Before everything had changed, and she had been hurt.

But Claire and I had just been friendly. Yes, I had found her attractive.

Just because I never allowed myself to see Claire in that way, didn't mean that somewhere deep down it hadn't been there. Waiting. Lurking. Especially for the most inopportune time.

Like when we were alone in a cabin in the woods in a snowstorm, where she needed to be able to trust me. And I needed to not be the asshole who got a hard-on whenever she was around. But those hips kept moving.

They were intoxicating. As if they were calling to me.

Maybe I should switch to water.

But then Claire moved forward, and clinked her drink to mine, and grinned.

"At least we're having fun, right? I'm sad the others aren't here." She tossed back half her old fashioned, and I winced, and realized maybe we both needed water. But then I had another drink, and realized maybe it was okay that we didn't.

Maybe it was okay that we just enjoyed ourselves.

There had been enough stress and heartache going on around us. So I was just going to let the bourbon do the talking and thinking for us all.

"These are really strong," Claire said, as she sank into the cushions of the couch next to me and let out a deep breath. "But it's good that they're strong. Because then it lets me forget about the fact our best friends are stuck back at home or at the bottom of the mountain because they can't get up here."

"We always knew that closing the pass was going to be a possibility," I said, trying to be adult about the situation. Only I was pretty sure I slurred a couple of those words. What did I know?

She smiled up at me and took another sip.

"I just feel bad. But I would feel worse if you were up here alone and I hadn't made it. Or if I was up here alone. And then I would have serial killer mountain dweller, Bigfoot worries."

I nearly snorted the bourbon and had to set down my glass for a second.

"Did you just call Mr. Sasquatch a serial killer?"

"Did you just call him Mr. Sasquatch?" she asked, those gorgeous eyes of hers widening.

I really needed to stop thinking of her eyes as gorgeous if I was going to make it through this night whole.

"We have to put respect on his name."

"I'm saying serial killer or Bigfoot. Or Sasquatch if that's what name you'd like to use."

"I just feel like that's what name he would like. Bigfoot sounds kind of derogatory."

"I thought if you had big feet, you had a big dick. Why would you think that was a bad thing?" She blinked at me slowly, before she pressed her lips together, her eyes comically wide.

"I really don't want to think about Mr. Sasquatch's dick."

"I'm pretty sure that's not a sentence you've ever thought you would say aloud in your life."

"There's really no going back from this."

"This is a ridiculous conversation."

"It really is. But there is security out here. It's sort of what my family does."

Her face sobered for an instant, and I could have cursed myself. *We* had had security in the apartment where she'd almost died before. And it hadn't been enough.

"I trust you guys. It's the whole woman living alone thing. Even before...well before that incident. But I'm just going to have another drink and I'm not going to think about this, okay?"

She said the words very quickly, so quickly that it took me a minute for me to understand them all.

"I'm so fucking sorry."

She put her hands to my mouth, my lips pressing against her skin. "No. You don't need to be sorry. It's over with and done—it's in the past."

"Claire," I whispered against her skin, and she pressed firmer. So I kissed her fingertips. I didn't mean to, it just felt like something I should do. When she froze for an instant, I realized that was probably a very bad idea.

Her fingers fell, and I felt bereft, but I didn't say anything. Instead I just stared at her, as she looked down at her hand, and then back up at me.

"Sorry."

"Claire..."

She shook her head. "Okay, so you'll protect me against Bigfoot. I mean Sasquatch. Good to know. However, I'm glad I'm not alone up here. Even the wind gets creepy in the trees when you're alone in a cabin in the woods. I'm pretty sure there is a serial killer. Or maybe like a monster."

"Other than Mr. Sasquatch?" I asked, playing into the joke.

"Other than him. Like the one from another dimension, or a portal that opens up and tries to take you into a hell dimension. You know, so we can go visit the guys from *Supernatural*."

"Why do you sound so excited about visiting the guys from *Supernatural*?" I asked dryly.

"I'm in love with Jensen Ackles. There I said it. I love him."

I let out a sad sigh. "We'll never live up to them, will we?"

"You really won't. But it's okay. He's happy in real

life, and totally not the guy who likes pie and screams when he sees a cat."

"You know I have no idea what any of that means."

She put her hand to her chest, and I did my best not to look at her breasts. "Are you kidding me right now? You don't know what I'm talking about?"

"Well not really. I've seen the memes. And all the videos."

"Wait. How is that even possible? I know that your cousins love the show. At least some of them."

"Well, I have like forty-nine cousins last time I counted. We haven't watched all the shows out in existence."

"But you have family jokes with the *Supernatural* lore," she pointed out.

I shrugged, feeling a little embarrassed. "I watched the first episode when I was younger, probably too young, and the lady on the bridge really scared the fuck out of me. It didn't help that Kane had been hiding behind a door and jumped out at me when I was going around the corner, and then also scared the shit out of me, and I did scream. Much like Jensen Ackles in that meme."

"Oh my God. Well we're going to have to watch it. I'm really sorry. But I'll hold your hand if you get scared. As long as you know you don't let the serial ax-wielding monster, Mr. Sasquatch, get me while we're here in the forest."

I looked at her and laughed, before taking another sip of my drink.

"Fine. But you have to hold me if I'm scared."

The snow continued to pound against the window, increasing in its ferocity, and I let out a breath, before she nodded, and went to turn on *Supernatural*.

We sat in the dark, and I tried my best to keep my heart from pounding, and it had nothing to do with the jump scares on the TV.

"I thought his voice was lower," I said, and Claire rolled her eyes and sighed deeply against me.

"I think his voice gets lower as the show moves on. I mean, it's Jensen Ackles, I'm pretty sure he just ended up with the Dean voice."

"You say that as if it's a thing."

"Oh it's a thing," she said with a dreamy sigh.

The fact that I could feel the warmth of her breath against my chest forced me to keep still.

Because she was leaning against me, both of us drinking a little too much, and both of us continuing not to care.

But maybe it was just the storm, and the mood, and nothing to do with where my mind was going.

When the first episode ended, and the boys got into that ridiculous car of theirs that had to eat up a tank of gas every ten minutes, she let out a happy sigh, and sat up.

I ignored the fact that I missed the feel of her body against mine instantly.

"Ready for round two?" she asked, and I nodded.

"Yeah, let me get a snack or something. Another drink?" I asked, knowing we both should probably stick to water.

But then she nodded, and I licked my lips.

I didn't miss the fact that her gaze went to the action, but I ignored it, or at least tried to. It was probably just me seeing things.

I went to make some popcorn, and on my way back in, Claire was standing, and stretching. She had her arms above her head, and I could see a sliver of her stomach as her shirt rode up. It also made her breasts rise, and I had to pull my gaze from them.

She was so damn beautiful. And there was seriously something wrong with me.

I cleared my throat and set the popcorn down.

"Okay. Is this a good enough snack?"

She nodded, and as we both reached down for the popcorn, our hands brushed, and she jumped back. Only I sort of jumped forward in an odd jerky motion, and then the popcorn was flying to the ground, as was she.

"Shit."

I gripped her hips to keep her steady, and of course that meant I was pressing her hips against my hips, and then she could feel everything.

Every single hard line of me.

She put her hands on my chest, keeping her steady, and then both of us were looking at each other, our breaths coming in pants, and both of us leaning to the side just a bit.

My mind was a bit blurry.

"Sorry."

I nodded, but didn't say anything, instead I did something monumentally stupid, and I reached out to cup her cheek, my thumb sliding along her cheekbone.

"No problem. I'm pretty clumsy."

"As clumsy as Mr. Sasquatch?" she asked, her voice a little breathy.

"I didn't realize that he tripped."

"If Mr. Sasquatch falls in the woods and nobody's around to hear, does he really fall?" she asked.

If she could come up with a sentence like that, maybe she wasn't as drunk as I thought, but either way, I had to make sure. At least before I made a stupid fucking mistake.

"Claire?"

"Kingston?"

"How much have you had to drink?"

"Just as much as you."

"So if I were to kiss you right now? Would that be a really big fucking mistake?"

"Probably? But I'm not drunk enough to regret it."

I took that as a yes, and so when I leaned forward and brushed my lips against hers, I couldn't help but relish the soft moan that escaped her lips.

She tasted of bourbon and cherry, with a touch of orange, and Claire.

And because I couldn't stop thinking of this, because I had ignored this moment for so long, I deepened the kiss, both of us groaning.

I should have pulled back. I should have laughed this off.

And yet, as the power flickered around us, and the snow began to fall in earnest, I just felt. I just let myself. When her hands slid up my shirt, her warm palms on my back, I growled.

"Tell me to stop," I whispered.

"Don't."

My lips quirked into a smile against hers, and then there was no thinking. I tugged her shirt off her, one quick motion that surprised us both, and then my thumbs were playing over the swell of her breasts, sliding between them to undo the front clasp.

Her eyes darkened, her pupils dilating as I met her gaze and undid the snap. Her breasts fell heavy into my palms, and she threw her bra to the side, as I leaned down to take one puckered nipple into my mouth, and then moved to the next. Her hand tightened in my hair as I continued to feast on her breasts; they were so firm, larger than my palm. I knew that one day I would want to fuck those tits, to suck on them until her nipples were hard cherries, and her flesh was covered in my marks. But not now. No, I needed all of her.

I let her tug off my shirt, and I tossed it over my head, as she raked her nails down my back, over my chest, as we continued to explore each other. I pulled down her leggings, and knelt in front of her, loving the way that her whole body blushed at the sight. We hadn't bothered to turn on the lights, so only the few candles and light from the TV shone on us, and maybe this was good. Maybe that was best for both of us. That meant I couldn't quite see in detail the scar that had changed everything. And I didn't want to think about that. Because I knew she didn't want to think about it either.

I kissed down her stomach, over her panties, and nuzzled her pussy. She let out a shocked gasp, her body shaking.

Mine.

I didn't say it. I wanted to. But damn it, she was *everything* in this moment.

I breathed hot air over her dampening panties before slowly, oh so slowly, sliding them over her hips. She was bare before me, a little triangle of hair on her mound. And it was all I could do not to bury my face between her legs and feast on that glorious cunt before me.

When I licked my lips and let her panties reach the floor, she kicked them to the side. Then I found myself kneeling in front of her, both of our breaths coming in pants. *We should probably stop.* Honestly, with her naked before me, and my dick so hard I could barely see straight, there was no going back.

"Tell me to stop. I'll stop right now. Tell me to stop."

I didn't know if I was begging her to stop, or to continue.

In answer, she nodded at me, and for an instant I thought it was a disappointment, before she slid her hands through my hair again.

"Don't stop."

As a man on a mission, I let out a feral snarl and feasted. I latched my mouth on her cunt, her sweet and tart juices coating my tongue. She let out little whimpers as I ate my fill, sucking on her clit, and using my tongue to dive deeper into that pussy of hers.

Her lips were swollen, her whole body shaking. So I kept one hand on her ass, keeping her steady as I pressed her to my face, and let her roll her hips to ride me.

I knew she came when her whole body shook, and

my mouth flooded with her arousal. I lapped up every single drop, as she panted my name, and then I was standing, crushing my mouth to hers. I needed her to taste herself on me, to need every ounce of me. I slid my jean-covered thigh between her legs, and she rode me, rubbing her clit on my thigh, leaving evidence of her wetness down my denim.

It was the single hottest fucking thing I had ever seen.

And then we were shoving off my jeans, and I sat down on the couch.

"Ride me. Let me taste those tits as you ride me."

Her eyes widened as she looked down at my cock, and I put one hand at the base, and gently slid it up to the tip, rolled my thumb over the pre-come there, and slid it back down.

"You can take me."

"I'm not quite sure I can take all of you," she said a little dryly, her lips swollen, her body red.

I just smiled like a man in fucking heaven. "Way to feed a man's ego."

"You're welcome?" She froze, her body shaking. "I'm on birth control but...it's not perfect," she whispered, and I cursed under my breath.

"Shit. I can't believe I forgot. I've got a condom in my wallet." She raised a brow. "It's always a smart thing."

"I have one in my purse. Even though I'd never planned on using it."

And at that moment there were far too many words between us, so I stood up, my dick pressed against her stomach, and kissed her again, needing her.

We had moved so fast, but this pause seemed to slow everything down. So instead I continued to kiss her, running my hands over her body, cupping her breasts. And when we slid the condom on, I let her do it, pumping me a few times before she squeezed the base of my dick.

I nearly saw stars, and then I was sitting, with her hovering above me.

"Take me. Take all of me."

Her eyes widened but she nodded. I knew the drink was still buzzing between us, and whatever else was going on. But I knew we wouldn't forget this in the morning.

I just didn't know why we were doing this, and why it had taken so long.

In that moment, when she slid down on my dick, her sweet pussy clamping down around my cock, I knew I didn't need any answers in the moment. Everything else could wait.

Instead she slowly, painstakingly sat down on me, her body stretching to fit me.

"Are you okay?" I asked, my hand on the back of her neck. "If I'm hurting you, let me know."

She shook her head, those beautiful eyes wide. "No, you're just really big."

"Thank you, baby." And I kissed her again, as she rolled her hips.

That action pulled moans out of both of us, so I used one hand to slide my thumb over her clit, as she rolled her hips and rode me. I kept my other hand on the back of her neck, my hands making a fist in her hair.

She was so fucking beautiful, an empress.

My empress.

And when she came again, clamping around my cock, I followed her into that temptation, into that bliss with no ending. I lowered her to me, keeping my mouth on hers, afraid of what words would come.

There were none, just feelings, just us.

And there was nothing else to say.

Just this moment. Just this promise.

I just held Claire...and hoped the drink would be enough for us to breathe again.

And we wouldn't run once morning came.

6

CLAIRE

Phoebe's voice echoed in my ears. *"Get out. Get help."*

I needed to push Tim out of the way. To stop him from holding my best friend by the neck and threatening us. Everything moved as if I were locked in ice, my feet stuck in cement as I continued to put one step after the other, and yet I couldn't move forward. There was a hollowness in me as I continued to reach toward the door, to leave my best friend behind and run for help. Because none of the fighting and plans we had made had worked until now at this point. There was nothing for us.

My apartment began to grow in size, the feet between Phoebe and I growing immensely until I could no longer see her, and then she was right next to me again, our fingertips brushing as she was screaming at me to get help.

Tim didn't have a face, just a darkness as he squeezed my best friend's neck and shook her, that silent predator who told me that what was to come would break us. I tried to open my mouth and scream, to beg the gods for help and yet nothing came. It felt as if wet paper were in my mouth, and I tried to pull it out, globs at a time, and yet there was nothing. I couldn't breathe, I couldn't move.

And then my toes were barely touching the ground, and it felt like I was flying, my back hitting the ceiling as I tried to swim through the air to get to help. I was out of Tim's reach, I would be safe, and I would save Phoebe. I swam through the air, doing my best to make it out, but then Tim was there, and Phoebe was on the ground, and though I couldn't see Tim's face, I could see his smile.

The Cheshire Cat grinned at me, eyes red slits as they glared, and then white-hot pain.

That odd sucking sound of knife sliding into flesh once, twice.

The blade cut deep, damaging something, and the warmth of blood slid down my side and through my fingers.

And I fell backward, falling, falling, until there was nothing left, just screams and echoes.

Were they my screams, or were they Phoebe's?

I wasn't sure. Because in the end, I tried to run for safety for us, because no matter how many times I had hit back, no matter how many times I had pushed and begged, there was nothing.

"Claire! Claire! Wake up."

My eyes shot open at Kingston's voice, and I realized that he was holding me, squeezing my arms to wake me up.

The echoes of my screams reverberated in my ears, and I realized I had been screaming. My throat was raw, and I swallowed hard, looking up at him.

"I screamed in your face," I muttered, my voice breaking.

"It's okay. I probably deserved it."

"*I screamed in your face,*" I repeated, this time my voice slightly lower.

Kingston stared at me for an instant before giving me a slight nod and pushing my hair back from my face. Everything felt sticky, as if I were covered in sweat, but I couldn't breathe, couldn't think.

Not with the memory of those dreams still flowing through my veins, and not with Kingston holding me.

"You're okay now. I've got you. I've got you, Claire."

There was such a strength in his words, and I wanted to believe him. With every ounce of my soul I wanted to believe him.

"I'm sorry. I don't usually have that many night-mares anymore."

Not quite a lie. Usually the dreams I couldn't wake up from. And then I would finally turn in my sleep and find a different dream. One a little sweeter, one possibly of Kingston himself.

And that's when I realized that I lay naked in his arms, my breasts pressed to his chest, and he was hold-ing me.

"I can feel your heartbeat," I whispered, wondering why that was the first thing that came to mind. My hand was on his chest, over the slight hair there, and the defined pecs I knew came from hours of working out and keeping his body toned for his job. He was all strength and muscle and part of me wanted to lean into that, to believe that it was safe.

And yet, I wasn't sure I was allowed to.

I could not believe that I'd slept with Kingston Montgomery. And now he was holding me, both of us naked, and I'd had a bad dream in front of him.

"How often do you have these nightmares?" he asked, still playing with my hair. I didn't move my hand, the other one off to the side so I wouldn't be tempted to touch him.

At some point during the night Kingston had moved us to his bed. Not mine, not to another bed, but *his*. We had fallen asleep on top of each other on the couch after we had had the hottest sex of my life. My thighs were still sore from the way he had held onto me, pounding into me from below me. It had been the single most erotic moment of my life, and I knew that no matter how many nightmares I had, perhaps just that moment with him would be enough to push some of those scary thoughts away.

Not all of them, as was evident by my nightmare, but some.

And that had to be enough.

"Do you want to talk about it?" Kingston asked, and I pulled myself from staring at his square jawline and back up to those dark blue eyes of his. I could only see the shadows of them because of the skylight that was now illuminated thanks to the moon bouncing off the fallen snow. He was far too beautiful for his own good.

"You know what it was about. You were there."

He closed his eyes and pressed his forehead to mine. For a moment, shame coated me. Because he had been there. He had held my body as I was bleeding out and pressed onto my wound so sharp pain had stuck its jagged claws through me. And I had survived, wondering if his gaze would be the last thing I saw.

So I looked into those eyes again, and reminded myself I was here.

"I wish we had been there sooner. I hated that we weren't. And that's such a paltry thing to say."

In that instant I realized I wasn't the only one holding shame here. Perhaps it was because we were already baring all, I felt the courage to reach out and slide my hand through his hair.

"You came. There was nothing you could have done."

"You can say that after the fact. But not so much during. It's not about me, anyway. This is about you."

Kingston sat up then, and I felt the loss of his touch, his heat. But then he did the most interesting thing and pulled me onto his lap. His very hard and thick cock pressed against my backside, but we both were determined to ignore it in that instant. I hadn't even realized I was still shaking from the dreams, and he held me close, running his hands up and down my sides.

When I didn't say anything, he let out a low breath. "I remember running up the stairs, trying my best to get there in time. I've never actually seen Kane run that fast."

"He ran for Phoebe." It wasn't a complaint. In fact, it brought warmth to my heart that Phoebe was so loved—so cared for.

"Yeah, he did."

I didn't ask who Kingston ran for. Just because I was sitting naked on his lap in this instant, didn't make me that person. But it did remind me that he had done what he could for us.

"I just hated the fact I couldn't do anything. I tried to push at him, to get out of that situation, and there was nothing I could do. We had all the security set up, and in the end, I stood there like a deer in headlights for too long, and then when I did fight back it wasn't enough."

I couldn't believe I was saying these words at this moment, but with the sound of the cool wind through the trees as the snowstorm had finally ended, I felt as if I could just breathe. Because we were slightly in the dark, and it was Kingston.

"You did everything right. You were smart. You were careful. He bypassed our security in a way that we didn't even think was possible."

"Because he killed our neighbor." My voice broke at the words, and he held me close, running his hands down my side.

"And because he crossed that line, and because he cut the power, he got in. We should have found a way to make sure that hadn't happened."

"It wasn't your fault. You protected us. Throughout all those weeks while we were waiting to see what would happen, you helped."

And I couldn't even fight back.

"I can teach you some self-defense if you want. Crew's better at it, because he does that on the side, but all of us are trained. If you'd rather Daisy or

Jennifer so you have a woman, they can help. Especially with some of the center of mass issues. But I'll show you a few things. I don't want to say for next time, because there's not going to be a next time. But I can help."

I looked up at him then and swallowed hard.

"Really?"

"I should have mentioned it before. But both of us were very good about not talking about any of this."

"And then there was the whole avoiding you thing."

He frowned at me. "You ever going to tell me why?"

Not exactly. But I didn't say that out loud. "I needed to find my footing."

He played with the end of my hair, his fingers brushing my bare shoulder. "And did you figure that out?"

I shook my head. "No. But I'm still here."

His cock twitched against my backside, and I swallowed hard, with reality finally settled in. We were both naked in his bed, all alone in a snowstorm, and I was sitting on his lap.

"I was wondering when you were going to realize exactly where you were sitting."

"Oh, I knew. And I felt."

"So you just weren't going to say anything. You were just going to sit on my lap for the rest of the night?"

"You're the one who put me there," I whispered.

Kingston grinned then, his eyes brightening. I loved when his eyes brightened. "Okay, I can out you somewhere else."

And then I was on my back, and my thighs were on his shoulders as he spread me before him. "So soft and pink."

"Kingston," I whispered.

"You tell me when to stop."

"Never." I hadn't meant to say that word. A truth so rich in secrets I knew it would break me, but when he met my gaze, his face between my thighs, his tongue so close to my pussy, there was nothing else I could say.

In answer he hummed against me, as he began to lick and suck at my clit. My toes curled, and I gripped the bedsheets, arching my back as he continued to eat me out. His tongue laved at me, and then he speared me with one finger, two, stretching me until I knew that I wouldn't be able to last much longer. When he curled his fingers and rubbed against that little bundle of nerves, I lost it. My hands going to my breasts to pinch my nipples as I came, riding his face with all abandon.

He went to hover over me but then I shook my head, twisting so I pushed him down on his back.

He let out a little grunt, as I laughed, I went to kneel between his legs. "Well, I see you have an agenda?" he asked, as he put his hands behind his head.

"I'm just saying. I didn't get to do this last time."

"Well, take your fill. Until it's my turn again."

I gripped the base of his cock, my fingers not touching, and licked my lips. He groaned, and I leaned down over him, my hair covering my face, as I licked the tip of his cock.

Salty pre-come settled over my tongue, before I opened my mouth and took the head of his cock in. His whole body shuddered, one hand going to my hair, the other reaching down to play with my nipple. He must have levered himself up somewhat on the pillow, but I let him touch me, because I needed him to touch me.

I bobbed my head, flattening my tongue as I let him fully into my mouth, pressing the back of my throat. And when I swallowed, letting him further back, he moaned.

"Dear God."

I didn't smile or say anything, mostly because his cock was in my mouth and I knew if I pulled back, he would probably pounce on me. And while I liked the thought of that, I wanted to give him something more. So I rolled his balls in one hand and continued to bob over him, letting him go past the back of my throat and deeper, taking him all the way in. My nose nuzzled the coarse hair at the base of his cock, and I hummed against him. His whole body shook as he tried his best to stay still, his breaths coming in pants as I did my best to breathe through my nose. And then I pulled back, panting, and met his wide gaze.

"Oh my God," he muttered.

"Did I mention I can swallow really well?" I teased.

"Well, I think we just became best friends." Laughing, I went back to him, taking more and more of him.

I continued my pleasure, loving the little grunts that came from him, and when he stiffened, his balls tightening in my hand, he pulled me away, and kissed me again.

"As much as I want to come down that pretty throat, or on those tits of yours, I really need to be inside you."

I nodded quickly as he went to the bedside table and pulled out condoms.

My brows raised.

"Well, this was originally supposed to be Kane's bedroom, so we're just not going to think about anything. Since I, you know, packed the house with him."

I laughed, grateful that we had that taken care of, and then I was on all fours in front of him, and he was gripping my hips.

"You tell me if it's too much."

"I trust you," I said, meaning every single word.

He kissed up my back, before he spread me again, and then there was nothing else. He speared me, pounding into me thrust for thrust until he was balls deep, and I was meeting him with each movement.

He pulled me up so my back was to his front, his one hand on my throat, the other on my breasts, and I continued to roll my hips against him, needing that sensation, needing him.

There was so much, and yet not enough, and I couldn't breathe.

And when I came around him again, he pulled out of me, and twisted me so I was on my back, and he was rolling his hips into me.

I wrapped my legs around his waist, and he cupped my cheek to kiss me softly.

"I'm almost there. I'm almost there, Claire."

"Finish. Take me."

He smiled his wicked smile, and then he was moving, and each of us meeting gazes, and never breaking.

And when he came, his mouth parting, I knew I was in deep trouble.

So he leaned down and took my lips, and I held onto him, meeting every inch of him.

As we finally settled, able to catch our breath, Kingston held me close, and smiled against my lips.

"So I suppose we should probably shower."

I blinked up at the odd choice of words.

"Oh?"

"Well, it just seems like we have a very large house, and an equally large box of condoms. I think a shower could be nice."

I just shook my head at him.

"Really? I didn't realize that your recovery is that good."

"Well, I'm sure there's something I can do while we wait. Just saying."

And I pushed all thoughts of what could happen, and what we should say to each other, out of my mind. We would deal with reality soon. For now, I would live in whatever dream this happened to be. Because it wasn't the nightmare that had woken me up. No, it was something that could lead to a break I didn't want to think about. But for now, it was just him, me, and whatever promises we didn't make.

After all, we only had one night. And I would take it.

SAMANTHA:

Thanks for visiting yesterday. You really perked him up.

ME:

Anything for Eddie. You know that. Plus I like visiting. You both make me laugh enough my sides hurt.

SAMANTHA:

We try. And thank your mom for me. She didn't have to make us so many dinners!

ME:

You know she wanted to. It's her thing.

SAMANTHA:

Bless you, Montgomerys.

ME:

Just get some rest and I'll see you
soon.

SAMANTHA:

You too.

"Are you ready to go yet?" Lex asked from my side, and I glared at my cousin as I put my phone on my dresser. I stood there in my towel after getting out of the shower and already wanted to be finished with this family event.

"Why do you say that as if you've been waiting for me for an hour. You're the one who got here ten minutes early."

"And you know the rules. Being on time is late, being ten to fifteen minutes early is on time."

"Honestly, you're early to my house so we could get to the course even earlier? The math ain't mathing."

"Just finish packing up your things. How hard can it be to figure out which polo shirt you want to wear?"

I glared at my cousin. Lex, AKA Lexington Mont-gomery was the son of my Uncle Beckett and Aunt Eliza. He'd been adopted into the family a couple of months after I was born, and we were the same age. We'd grown up together in the ways that cousins tended to, though we didn't attend the same schools since I was in Boulder for most of my childhood, and then down in Denver when we'd moved down for my dad's art. Lexington had lived up in Fort Collins his entire life, but the thing with Colorado was that even though we lived in different cities, it all felt the same. Driving an hour up north to Fort Collins wasn't anything, we would do it weekly if not more. The I-25 corridor was great for that, and getting to Boulder was a snap. That's why even though all of my cousins had been spread out over the suburbs of Denver and each of the major cities surrounding it, we all were thick as thieves and close as ever.

It wasn't like when we visited Lex's cousins down in Texas where everything was spread out to the point that driving to another city would take four to eleven hours. No, we were lucky that way. Hence why people would joke that the Montgomerys were taking over the world. We happened to have a higher percentage of people in this state than one would think.

"When did you ever see a Montgomery in a polo shirt?" I asked, annoyed.

"Hey, huge football players and celebrities go golfing all the time. They wear polos. We all can't be Adam Sandler in a T-shirt and large athletic shorts."

I snorted, shaking my head at Lex. "Maybe I should go dressed as Adam Sandler."

"Or you could just put on a polo and some khakis and pretend like you know what you're doing."

I flipped the other man off and walked in a towel toward my closet. I had khakis and a polo for instances like this, or for events where I needed to blend in with the clientele. But it wasn't usually my favorite thing. Give me jeans, gray sweatpants, and a Henley? I was fine.

"How much ink do you think is going to be on our course today?" I asked with a laugh.

"Enough that we'll scare the locals. I'm going to really enjoy it. Especially when Crew comes around with all his piercings."

The Montgomerys and friends were headed to the golf course today, and I wasn't quite sure why I had agreed to it. But they wanted to go, so we were going to figure out how to be adults. Apparently. We needed activities to do as friends and family that didn't involve throwing axes or playing video games apparently. At least, that's what my mother had said jokingly over dinner one day, and now here we were.

Lex continued to talk behind me, as I found a polo shirt that I didn't mind wearing, this one charcoal gray. I would just have to wear some form of cream or white pants, I thought I had some at least. I still didn't know why we were going golfing, but I was just going to roll with it.

Plus doing something out of the ordinary seemed to be what I was good at recently.

Considering that I had slept with Claire.

And it hadn't been just one time. It had been numerous times over the night. We hadn't slept at all, except for a few dozing naps with each other, and there was no going back. I could still feel the softness of her skin underneath my fingertips—could still feel her clamping around me as she came.

Then there was the way that the side of her mouth quirked up into a smile, while the other side would scrunch just slightly so it looked like she always had something on her mind, a little mischievous.

There was seriously something wrong with me. Because I felt as if I had studied every inch of her, multiple times, and I was still getting to know her, finding new aspects that drew me in.

And here I was, waxing poetic nonsense and shit as if I knew what I was doing. This was not like me. But hell, nothing I had done with Claire was like me.

The morning after, we had woken up from our catnap, packed our things up, checked out the house, and then said our goodbyes. It had been awkward, and yet, not as awkward as it could have been. As it should have been.

We had both said we would see each other soon, and I had tucked her hair behind her ear, and she smiled up at me. And then we'd parted ways.

We hadn't discussed anything. About what we

would do when we saw each other next or what we would say. For all I knew she was telling Phoebe and all the Montgomery girls exactly what happened. And here I was, not telling anybody, because I had no idea what I was thinking, or what was going to happen next.

Total mature shit.

I got dressed, ignoring the way that Lexington rolled his eyes when I just dropped towel in front of him. If the man didn't want to see my ass, he could have just left the room. I pulled on boxer briefs, and then white khaki-feeling golf pants, and then shoved on the polo.

"Look at you, all fancy now. You're going to get grass stains on those pants."

"Are you saying I'm going to trip and fall?" I grabbed my bag and gestured toward Lex. "Let's go. I still can't believe that only a couple of days after a fucking snowstorm we're going golfing, but here's Colorado weather for you."

"We don't look a gifted sunny day in the eyes. That's the whole thankfulness of living in this weird state."

"I don't think any of what you said was part of the actual metaphor or simile. I'm just saying."

"Actually I think it's just an idiom. Like a cultural thing. We probably should have taken more English classes."

I laughed. "Well I don't need no English. I just sit there and grunt and look fierce."

"And I just hit a hammer against a nail and really hope the house doesn't fall down."

Lexington, along with a few other cousins, had joined up with Montgomery Inc, but Inc, not Ink. They had eventually broken off into a subsidiary, called Montgomery Inc Too. They still were under the major family umbrella like all of us were, but instead of working on all the same projects with their parents and uncles and aunts, much like the tattoo shops, they had branched off into their own.

I liked the fact that there were so many handy people in my family. Sure, I could do a few things on my own, but not everything. And while we didn't take freebies and handouts, we did trade and barter our services. Meaning any home improvement projects I wanted done at my house, I could get at cost, or for just helpful hints when it came to security and installation.

It all worked out in the end.

"So, did you have fun up in the lodge with Claire?" Lex asked as I got into the passenger seat, and we made our way toward the course.

I tried my best not to look as if I were guilty. Because there was nothing to be guilty about. We hadn't done anything wrong.

It was just I had no idea what we had done in terms of labels and the grand scheme of things, and I didn't want to talk about it. Part of me wanted to shout from the rooftops, but that sounded like a bad idea.

So I wouldn't. I would just pretend nothing had happened. And I had been silent for a little too long.

"It snowed worse down at the base where they closed the pass than it did up where we were. It was weird, but I guess we were on the opposite end of the storm. So we got some snow, but then the roads were fine by the time we drove the next morning."

"What did you guys do, play video games or something?"

"Yeah, a little bit. Watched a movie. Drank too many old fashioneds." Had hot sex multiple times throughout the cabin.

"I love that she loves bourbon."

My lips quirked into a smile. "She makes a better old fashioned than I do, I had to steal a recipe."

"Oh, I want it too," Lex said as he pulled off the highway.

"She learned it at a mixology class actually. She learned a few things."

"You can take classes for that?" Lex asked, and then shook his head. "Of course you can. People need to learn to be bartenders rather than watching somebody make Jack and Cokes."

"That is the max ability of some of our family members though," I said with a laugh. "And she needed to learn it for some party or something. I don't really remember."

Of course I remembered. I remembered everything about Claire. But that made me sound stalkerish. And this wasn't like me.

"That's cool. I forget that she plans parties. Big ones or just like kids' birthday parties?"

"Big ones. Although I know she does some parties that are birthday-like. And even weddings. She's growing leaps and bounds."

"She and Phoebe are both amazing when it comes to their businesses. I'm glad that Kane hooked up with Phoebe. I like them."

"Oh?" I asked, noticing the slight twinge of jealousy I needed to get rid of.

"Yeah. Claire's fun. I'm glad that she's around more, since I know she sort of hid away after everything that happened."

I gritted my teeth and let out a deep breath. "Yeah. But she's back."

"That's good. Maybe I'll see what she's up to."

"Oh?" I asked, and Lex just snorted and shook his head. "There's a spot over there," I said, pointing to a very obvious parking spot, and trying to deflect the fact that I was not hiding my feelings and jealousy well.

Well shit.

Thankfully Lexington didn't ask any more questions,

probably because he got all the answers he needed, and I hated myself a little bit.

We got our clubs out of the back of the SUV, although I was borrowing one of my dad's sets because I didn't actually own any. And we made our way toward the rest of the group.

Leif and Nick would be partners, while Lex and Sebastian worked together. Noah and Ford were partners of course, and that left me with Crew, who was technically the only non-Montgomery of the bunch. But as he'd once dated Daisy, and was now all of our friends, it all made sense that he would be with us. In fact, Crew and Lexington hung out more often than not. They were always by each other's sides, and credited Daisy for that fact. And that's why the two of them weren't allowed to play together, because they could kick all of our asses.

So I had the pierced and tattooed man in a similar outfit to mine, who just raised that pierced brow.

"So how was your weekend?"

I shrugged, trying my best and failing to act nonchalant. "Snowy."

"Hmm."

I Ignored his pointed cough, as we set out to playing. I wasn't very good, but I was getting better. Thankfully I could mimic what Crew was doing, so it wasn't that bad.

Halfway through Crew gave me a once-over and smiled. "Well, well."

I looked over my shoulder and realized that the rest were paying attention to something else, and no one was looking at us. I leaned over and whispered fiercely. "How did you know?"

Crew just beamed and wiped his hand on his shirt. "I just know things." Then he gave me a look, raising that pierced brow. "So what are you going to do about it?"

"I have no fucking clue." It was the most honest thing I could have said in that situation because I wasn't sure what I was supposed to do.

I had always put Claire in a box, a friend of a friend, someone that I couldn't get near because if I fucked it up, it would hurt Phoebe and that would hurt Kane. The fact that Kane wasn't here today was helpful because he could read me like no other. Yes, Crew and Lex seemed to have read me just fine, but Kane? He would know. And then I would have to figure out what I was supposed to say. And yet here I was, trying to do the same.

"Well shit," Crew mumbled. "Claire's a nice girl."

"Woman," I corrected, and Crew nodded.

"Woman. She's *nice*. She's been through shit, but then again, so have you. Mister 'I got blown up in a warehouse and nobody likes to talk about it.'"

I winced. "Daisy was *in* the warehouse. I was just near it and got blown off my feet. We're both fine."

I could still remember the heat of it, the impact as I fell. Daisy had been hurt significantly more than I had but was back to her normal. I had been through another bomb, and a few knife wounds, and a bullet graze. All because I was in the job of protecting people. It wasn't safe, not always, but it was my job to make it safe.

Most days it was paperwork and installing cameras. Boring, and didn't give me the adrenaline that I needed, but it was enough.

But Claire? She had been hurt. On my watch. And that was something that was always going to be between us.

"Just figure something out, okay?"

I nodded, then remembered something that had happened that night. "Hey. You know that gym that you work at sometimes? Do they have open hours for one-on-ones?"

Crew nodded, a frown on his face. "Yeah, though you have a gym of your own, Mr. Montgomery."

I grinned. "Yeah, I do. But maybe I don't want to be working out right where my entire family's watching all the time."

Crew raised a brow. "Well, well. Things are going to get interesting."

And then it was his turn, and I stood back, and pulled out my phone without thinking.

ME:

Hey, I have a place we could work out if you want to work on those self-defense lessons. No pressure.

Well, that wasn't exactly what I had wanted to say right away, or how I'd wanted to reach out, but it was a good excuse.

CLAIRE:

Okay. Just tell me where. And when I guess. And what I'm supposed to wear. And well, I guess I'm going to need a long list.

She ended it with the laughing emoji, and my lips quirked.

ME:

I'll take care of you. I promise.

Before she could say anything to that, or I could think too hard, I texted again.

ME:

How are you?

Three little dots appeared quickly, then went away, then came back.

Well hell. Maybe on a golf course surrounded by family wasn't the best place to have this conversation over text.

CLAIRE:

Is this where we talk about the thing we're not talking about?

I threw my head back and laughed and ignored everyone staring at me for answers. Leif came over to read over my shoulder, and I pulled the phone away before he could see who it was.

"Ooh. I want to know."

"Privacy. Just a little bit."

"We're Montgomerys, we don't believe in privacy," Sebastian said, and I flipped him off, ignoring the fact that we were on a fucking nice golf course, and kept the phone to myself. Thankfully Crew seemed to be blocking people coming my way, and I would have to thank him again. Or it was possible I owed him more and more with each passing moment.

ME:

Maybe. If that's what you want.

How the hell had I missed that she was so cute and funny over these past months? Oh, because she was Phoebe's friend and that meant off limits. And maybe we had already crossed that line.

CLAIRE:

Maybe we should keep not talking about it? How many double negatives were in that?

ME:

If that's what you want. Or I can ask what you're wearing.

Shit, what the hell was I doing?

CLAIRE:

LOL. I'm wearing nothing but an apron. Barefoot in the kitchen.

My cock thickened, and I willed it down since these pants hid nothing. Crew cleared his throat beside me and I tilted a bit, annoyed at my own body's reactions.

ME:

Sure, darling.

CLAIRE:

I'm in leggings and a T-shirt as I am working on a plan for a welcome home party. Lots of things to do, and I feel so fancy right now.

ME:

I'm currently in a polo shirt and white khakis.

CLAIRE:

Oh my God. So fucking sexy.

ME:

I know, right?

CLAIRE:

Is this weird?

I nodded at Lex as he walked past me, interest in his gaze, but I ignored him again.

ME:

Yes, but I don't mind it.

CLAIRE:

I don't mind it either. But I guess I'll see you soon? Just don't get hit with any balls.

Before I could even text back, Claire texted first.

CLAIRE:

I meant golf balls.

ME:

I'll do my best.

CLAIRE:

I'll talk to you soon?

ME:

Yeah. See you soon.

Not exactly what she had said. Because we weren't just going to talk. I was going to see her. Maybe it was just going to be for a self-defense lesson. Maybe it was going to be more.

I had no fucking clue.

Crew looked over my shoulder, and I hadn't even realized the man had moved, before he whistled through his teeth.

"Fuck off," I growled. "I wasn't like this when you were dating Daisy."

Crew just laughed, and I was grateful that no one else was around us in that moment. "First off, I didn't realize you were *dating* Claire."

"Fuck. I'm not. That's not what I meant."

Crew just shrugged. "Well, choice of words and all that. But the reason that you weren't like this, the reason that you didn't hover over me when I was texting Daisy? Because Daisy can easily kick my ass and I was fine with that. And plus, I'm not going to get all growly over you with Claire. Nor are you going to ever need to worry about me with another Montgomery. That was a one and done."

I just shook my head. "Famous last words."

Crew glared. "Seriously, I'm never dating another Montgomery."

I just fluttered my eyelashes. "How could you? There's just so many of us. You can't just walk away."

Crew let out a laugh, then leaned forward, and

smacked a kiss to my lips. "Fine. I'll fuck you if that's what you want."

We both burst out laughing, as Lexington came over and looked between us. "So, what did I miss?"

And as we ignored him, and my other cousins came over, confusion on their faces even as they laughed, we went back to the game, and nobody asked me about my texting again. And yet all I could do was think about Claire, and exactly what the hell I was supposed to do when it came to her.

8

CLAIRE

"**A**unt Claire! Aunt Claire!"

I looked over as James ran toward me, his chestnut-colored hair shining under the sunlight, as Evelyn outpaced him.

Both seven years old, as fraternal twins they only vaguely resembled each other at this age. Evelyn looked so much like my brother, and therefore me, it was a little shocking each time I saw her. It was like watching a mini-me running toward me. James? He looked just like his mother.

I missed his mother with every ounce of my soul. She had been a kind woman, who had cared for her two kids, and had loved my brother. Fate wasn't kind most times, as I knew all too well.

But now these little kids, who weren't that little

anymore at seven years old, were running to me, with Evelyn's long legs pounding into the dirt, and James coming up from behind to beat her by an inch.

Evelyn had the sprinting, but James had the endurance. At least for now. Evelyn was an inch taller than James, and I knew that annoyed him to no end. It would change though, because despite looking like his mother, his growth spurts were just like his father's. My brother had been short for much of his youth, until sophomore year, and he shot up, surprising us all.

Now he was a six-foot-three behemoth of a man covered in tattoos and a full beard. In other words, he fit in with his new bosses, the Montgomerys, just fine.

I thought it a little weird that he had decided to work with the family that I had become friends with for so long, but in the end, the Montgomerys were the best in the business and my brother wanted to work with the best.

"Aunt Claire, tell him that he's wrong."

I raised my brow at my niece, then looked over at my nephew. "What are you wrong about?" I teased, and he gave me a put-upon sigh which meant I said the right thing.

"I'm not wrong. But I need you to make sure that she's wrong."

I barely followed that sentence. "So what are we fighting about now?"

The twins didn't truly fight often. They squabbled like any siblings, but it was them against the world. It had grown more so after losing their mother, and I knew that tragedy had shattered something in this family. My parents and I were trying to fill that void, but we weren't their mother. And my brother was doing his best at raising them alone. Of course, now that he was working for the Montgomerys, he wasn't alone. There was always childcare in the wings, and countless people to help if he was running late and my parents or I couldn't pick up one of the kids from one of their countless practices.

He had not only gotten a job, but he had gotten a second family, and for that I was grateful.

"She says that the original *Star Wars* was actually number four. And not number one. Why would they even release it that way? It makes no sense."

I blinked at James, then over at Evelyn, and wondered why this was what they were fighting about. "Your sister is right."

Evelyn smirked. "Ha. Told you."

"You couldn't tell from the different effects? I mean, there's a not-so subtle difference in all of the effects if you look at each trilogy. Or even the animated series and TV shows and single movies within that world."

Yes, I was a *Star Wars* geek, and I was a Trekkie. I refused to choose. I also liked *Babylon 5*, though nobody ever really asked. Only *Battlestar Galactica* was where I really shone. Katee Sackhoff as Starfire was my awakening. I knew right then and there I could marry a man or a woman and be just fine. But in reality I just wanted to marry Katee Sackhoff. I had said this to my brother once and he had just laughed, and agreed, that Katee Sackhoff especially as Starfire transcended any choices or desires.

My nephew scoffed. "All of the special effects were bad. I mean, nothing beats what's out now. I just thought they just didn't have the budget or something in the middle, then got it again in the end." James shrugged, and the two ran off, apparently to find something to play with a lightsaber with.

"Be careful!" I called out, as they crunched through the light snow.

It had been perfectly sunny the day before, hence why Kingston had been out golfing with his friends and family. But then we'd gotten a slight snowstorm the night before, and here we were, playing lightsabers and duels in the backyard. Colorado weather was interesting.

"I see that they're finally taking a hold of your nerdship."

I glared at my big brother as Hudson wrapped his arm around my shoulder. "You're the one who gave me the movies to begin with."

"Yes, but then you went off to write fan fiction."

"Let's not talk about my fan fiction. No one needs to know about it."

Hudson smirked. "So Phoebe doesn't know?"

I blushed, leaning into him. "No. And she doesn't need to know."

"I thought you didn't keep secrets between friends."

I ducked my head so he couldn't see me react, as those weren't the only secrets I was keeping from Phoebe. I was going to see Kingston later today, for self-defense training yes, but to see Kingston. And I didn't know exactly what I was going to say or how I was supposed to react around him. We had purposely not talked about what it all meant, and yet we had in a sense. Because we were going to see each other. And we wanted to.

And things were weird but nice. And maybe that was going to be enough.

Maybe it had to be enough.

"You're getting all lost in your thoughts again. You doing okay, little sister?"

I leaned into him and sighed. Yes, I had gone through hell recently, but so had he, so I didn't need to rehash all my problems with my big brother. He would want to carry my weight and the world's on his shoulders, but I wasn't going to let him.

Not today.

"I'm good. It's good to see them out and playing."

"Yeah. It is." His voice was a little gruff, and I rested my head on his shoulder, as he watched his children laugh as if they didn't have a care in the world, even though I knew it was the opposite.

But that wasn't about now. Yes, the real world hurt, and yes, there was always going to be some part that always ached, but my niece and nephew were resilient, and I had to credit most of it to their father. My brother was a good man, and he'd fought through hell to stand where he was right now.

"You're giving me that look," he whispered.

"What do you mean?"

"The one where you're rhapsodizing about how I am still here and breathing."

I winced. "I'm sorry."

"Don't be. I do the same thing every time that I look over at you and picture you in the hospital. The hospital that it took me way too long to get to."

"You didn't live here at the time. It's not your fault."

"I beg to differ, little sister. I should have found a way to get here."

I leaned into him a bit more. "You're here now. What more do I need?"

"Maybe a life."

"Hey. I was just thinking about how great you are, and now you're all mean to me."

Hudson moved to study my face and raised a single brow. I hated that he was so good at that look. Our dad had the same look and used it on both of us often. "Little sister, you need a life."

"I don't know what you're talking about. I have a life," I somewhat lied.

"You say that as if it's the truth. But I don't believe you."

"Let me be, okay? I'm fine."

"You know what *fine* stands for."

"That you just need to leave me alone and let me wallow?" I asked.

"Wallow in what?"

"Life and the lack of good coffee sometimes unless I go to my favorite cafe."

Hudson smiled, though I knew he was placating me. "I really do like that cafe."

I laughed, knowing it's what he wanted and honestly, what I felt. "It helps that you work right next to it. I have to drive to it."

"Oh God forbid you come and visit me."

"We both know I'm visiting the coffee."

He kissed the top of my head, then ran off to go chase his kids, and I just sighed, and watched them giggle and move around. I was so grateful for them, even if it sometimes felt I was the one on the outside looking in.

But sometimes I just wanted this for myself. Just a little bit.

I said my goodbyes, and hugged the kids as they decided which fake lightsaber they wanted to use and made my way to a gym about twenty minutes from my house. It wasn't too far, and I knew that while it wasn't necessarily owned by Crew, he went there often. At least that's what Kingston had mentioned.

I also knew that the Montgomery Security had its own private gym, but we weren't going there. I was oddly grateful. Even if it felt a little bit like hiding, I didn't want anyone else to see. And not just because this was with Kingston. Okay, most of it was because it was with Kingston. But I also didn't want them watching me do this. And failing.

I was probably going to fail spectacularly.

I pulled out my gym bag, complete with towel and water, and hoped what I was wearing was enough. After all, I had been wearing comfy clothes when I had been attacked before, and that hadn't helped. So maybe I should have worn like a dress or something. So I wasn't wearing leggings and a sports bra with a tank top and jacket over it. That wasn't the sexiest thing. Of course Kingston had seen me naked, so perhaps it didn't matter what I wore?

Why was I overthinking this so much?

There was a knock at my window, and the scream

that reverberated inside the cabin of my car could have split an eardrum, namely mine.

Kingston held up both hands, and I was grateful that he was the calm one in this situation, because this was probably not the best way to start a day of self-defense. As in I was so zoned out sitting here that I hadn't even realized a man had come to my window.

I opened the door when he stepped back and could feel the flames licking at my face.

"You didn't hear that, did you?" I asked, my voice slightly high-pitched.

"Are you asking if your car is soundproof? No. But I liked that you didn't panic." He pressed his lips together, holding back a laugh.

I rolled my eyes, and then froze as he leaned down and pressed a kiss to my lips.

It seemed so natural, as if we had done it a hundred times, and as he pulled back, he had a questioning look in his eyes.

"Okay?"

I pressed my fingers to my lips, and then looked up at him and nodded. "Yes. Okay."

"Good. I'm already fucking awkward, you know, with the whole making you scream thing." He paused and gave me a devilish look. "Except for that one time. Or seven times."

"You counted?" I asked as I closed the door behind me.

"As if you didn't?"

I blushed, and hip-checked him. Of course I just bounced right off him, and he reached out to catch me.

"Careful there."

"I have no idea if this whole you teaching-me-how-to-defend-myself is going to work. Considering you're just so..." I waved at him with my free hand. "Big."

"Seriously, you're going to have to stop with the compliments."

"I wasn't talking about your dick." At his wide gaze, I continued quickly. "Not that your dick isn't big. Because oh my God, so sore still. Well, I was for a while. However, I'm just going to stop talking right now because I'm talking really quickly, and I feel like if I don't take a breath right now, I might just run into that wall and just let what happens happen."

"I love when you get flustered, because you don't think about anything else. No stress, no worry about what's to come. I'm going to have to fluster you more often."

"Really?"

"Really."

We entered a gym that felt like one of those old school ones, with a boxing ring in the corner, a few bags around, and other equipment I couldn't name. It didn't smell like feet though, so I counted that as a win. We entered a side room, as we passed a few people who were working out, and I was grateful that this one seemed to be private.

"This is all ours, and it's going to be locked. That way nobody can see what we're doing, unless we want them to but there's no cameras in here because it's Crew's personal one. So you're safe from peeping Toms, but you are alone with me. So, is that going to be okay?"

"It's okay as in I feel completely safe with you. Probably not okay because we should most likely discuss at least something."

"What do you want out of this?" My eyes widened as my thoughts went directly to what *this* could be. Us? Life? Today? Kingston winced. "I meant this lesson."

"I totally knew that."

When he reached out and pushed my hair behind my ear again, I shivered. "You should stop doing that if we're going to focus."

"We can do that. Now, let's talk about it."

"I just want to make sure that what happened never happens again."

"I promise you I'm going to do all in my power to make that a reality."

I swallowed hard and nodded, knowing he was as serious as he could be. Because he still blamed himself, just like I blamed myself for trying to get help and leaving Phoebe behind.

Guilt was an enigma, that wrapped around you and never let you go, even when you thought you were finally free from it. But it continued to drown you, pound you against the rocks, and make you believe that you were worthless.

"The first thing you need to understand is it's not your fault."

It was if he read my mind, and I shook my head. "Just like it wasn't *your* fault."

He cleared his throat, and took a step back, and I tried to not think of that as rejection, but just us focusing on matters at hand.

"Situational awareness is key to everything. And well, what happened to you isn't exactly the same thing, being aware of your surroundings at all times is the first step."

"And I like to daydream."

"Well when you're walking with me, I'll be the one on alert."

"That has to be exhausting."

He shook his head. "No. It's just what my brain does. It's why I'm good at my job. But if you're walking by yourself, make sure you're aware of your surroundings. Don't walk with your headphones on, staring at your phone, not paying attention to the rest of the world. And I'm not even talking about what we're here for. It could be tripping over a curb or going out into traffic. I just don't want you to get hurt."

"That is true, and I always keep one earbud out, just so I can hear people coming up from behind me."

"So there you go, you're already a step ahead."

"That's true."

"Now the first things we're going to talk about are the five A's, which is what I was taught when I was a kid."

"The five A's?"

"Awareness, alertness, avoidance, anticipation, and action. The five A's."

"That sounds like a lot of words."

"True, but you've got this."

He went over each, and I swallowed hard knowing that this was for a good reason. "We can talk about your house in general, because I know that the others put up your security systems, but I can go through it again with you."

Kingston always did so much for me. Hell, for everyone in his circle. No matter how he was feeling or what he needed in his personal life, he always set that aside to help those he cared about.

And he cared about *me*.

Yet I'd run from him. I'd hid because I'd been scared. Not because of Kingston himself, but because of what he'd seen. Who I'd been when I'd been scared. And Kingston needed to know it wasn't him. It was *me*.

"I didn't blame you, that's not why I didn't answer my phone. That's not why I pushed you away."

"You ever going to tell me why?"

And that would be telling my feelings, but I'd already let him inside of me, so why couldn't I do this?

"Because I had a crush on you," I said point blank, knowing that if I could be strong here, I could be strong anywhere. His eyes widened, and I wanted to kick myself.

"You had a crush on me. As in past tense? So you pushed me away."

I ran my hands through my hair, annoyed when I forgot that I had already had my hair in a ponytail. "It's not that. It was more that I was going through a thousand things at once, and I needed to get over a crush, when it clearly wasn't reciprocated."

"I wouldn't say clearly."

"And yet you did nothing, and you never looked at me like that until recently."

"Because you were Phoebe's friend, and you were off limits."

I exhaled. "I'm not off limits anymore?"

"Well, now I'm breaking the rules, and we're going to have to deal with the consequences if there are any."

"There won't be. At least not with them. They're our friends."

"Then why haven't you told Phoebe?"

"How do you know I haven't?"

He smirked. "Because Kane would've told me."

"Maybe Phoebe wouldn't have told Kane because it would've been between us, or if she did share with her significant other, maybe he didn't share with you."

He shook his head, letting out a breath. "This is too fucking complicated."

"So maybe we shouldn't make it so complicated. Whatever this is."

"You're right. But that means we actually have to have answers."

"You got me on that one."

He leaned down and brushed his lips against mine. "How about we just work on keeping you safe?"

I nodded and fell into step next to him. I followed his moves, tried my best to put my thumb where it was supposed to when I punched out, and knew this was only day one. In the end I was sweaty, a mess, and had my back pressed to him, with his arms around me, only I was trying to get out of his grip, and it wasn't working.

"You can do this."

"I really can't."

I wiggled my butt, trying to get out, and Kingston groaned.

"Well, that's one way to do it." And that's when I felt the hard length of him against my backside, and I swallowed hard.

"Oh."

"Oh. Me holding you like this right now, this has nothing to do with self-defense, okay?" he asked, and his hold changed infinitesimally. And suddenly he was holding me softly, his hand sliding down my hip, and I groaned.

"Well, this is one way to end the lesson."

"Sounds like it."

He slid his hand over my leggings, in between my legs over the seam. It pressed me just right that I let out a shocked exhale of air.

"This room isn't soundproof," he whispered against my neck.

"Oh."

He rubbed against me, his hand underneath my tank top and over my sports bra, the other between my legs. I pushed back against him, rubbing along his length, as we both groaned. We weren't touching skin to skin, but it was one of the most erotic positions of my life.

Pent up, eager, I arched for him, wanting more, nearly at the edge, when his phone buzzed.

He cursed under his breath, and stopped, kissing the side of my neck.

"That's the emergency line."

Still thrumming, my heart racing, I nodded, and pulled back, bending over to take gulps of air.

Kingston's gray sweatpants were tented in the front, the lead pipe between his legs swinging to and fro. I really wanted to know why the man wasn't wearing underwear, but then again, I did not need to think about that.

Kingston frowned when he read the readout, his face graying a bit, as he answered. "Samantha, is everything okay?"

It would make sense that Samantha would be one of the ringtones that got through for emergencies. As we were still waiting on the final results for the bone marrow transplant, we were all on edge.

I was already moving toward him as his face fell, and he kept nodding even though I knew Samantha couldn't see.

"When?" A clipped word, and yet it spoke of so much.

My heart shattered, the world feeling as if it screeched to a stop as Kingston stood there, his face stoic, his jaw tight.

"Thank you for letting me know. I'm so sorry, Samantha. Yes. Yes. I'll be there. I'll get all the information. The team will be there too. You won't be alone. Is your family with you? Good. They'll handle things too. Sit down, Samantha. Drink some water. I'm so sorry." He ended the call, and stared at me, his eyes wide, bleak. "Eddie died. He threw a clot during the final procedure and he's... gone. Just like that, I couldn't save him. *He's gone.*" His voice broke, and when he fell to his knees I was there, holding him close to me.

"I'm sorry. I'm so sorry."

"I thought we could save him. I thought it was going to work this time." He kept repeating it, my shirt growing wet with his tears, and I cried into his hair, holding him close, knowing that there was nothing I could do to make anything better.

In his mind and heart, Kingston needed to save people. It was in his blood. It was his purpose. And he couldn't save his friend. It didn't matter that it was medicine, and cancer, and such a small percentage of success, Kingston had given everything he could, and it hadn't been enough against cancer.

In this moment, there was nothing I could do, nothing I could say, so I held him, and let the strong man who had just protected me, and taught me how to protect myself, fall into a million pieces and break.

9

KINGSTON

"Eddie Walker Silver lived a life of joy, love, and strength. And he died as he lived, in the arms of his doting wife, under the care of those who wanted to see him thrive, and under the strength of his own perseverance. We do not say he lost a battle. For this is not losing. This is merely an outcome that nobody wanted. He did not lose his fight, for that would outweigh the battle he clawed his way with bravery through. Eddie Walker Silver was a man of love and devotion. And he will be missed."

I squeezed Claire's hand after the speaker continued on about Eddie's power, his multiple awards in life, and everything that he had lived through.

I hadn't seen Eddie day-to-day in our lives. We hadn't worked together but he would come in the building with Samantha for her tattoos, and both would come in for coffee and sweet treats at the cafe. They'd even attended an art exhibit at the art gallery on the other end of the building. They had bought a piece of my cousin's art.

No, Eddie and I hadn't been best friends, nor did we share each other's deepest, darkest secrets. But our lives had been entwined in a way that you were with strangers who hadn't realized how close you could be. And I had bled for him and had tried to save him. I had tried to do so much.

Only a single blood clot had changed the game.

The next person stood up to speak, then Samantha, then Eddie's father, another friend, and then another.

And now I was supposed to sit here as the others spoke of Eddie, holding Claire's hand as Eddie's family —as well as mine—watched, and pretend that I could be as strong as the man who now lay in ashes in front of us. A wooden box carved for him by his grandfather. A grandfather who still lived and sat there with his chin up high as if he could fight back the tears with just a glare.

My friend lay in a wooden box, ashes to ashes, dust to dust, and it was all I could do not to scream.

Failed.

The match had failed. The treatment had failed. *I* had failed.

And then Samantha looked at me, and I cleared my throat, knowing what had to come next.

I turned to Claire and pressed my forehead against hers. It wasn't fair to rely on her like this, to need her strength. We didn't even know what we were to each other, and yet she was there for me. So I would be selfish in this instant and take whatever I could. I needed to be the strong one for Samantha and Eddie's family. If his grandfather could sit there with his chin held high, I could do the same.

"You've got this," Claire mouthed, and I nodded tightly, before standing fully and making my way down the aisle. I passed my parents, all three of them sitting together, with my mother sitting between them, holding both of my dads' hands. She gave me a tight nod, and I knew it was because she was ready to cry but wanted to hold back so she wouldn't weep. They'd gotten to know Eddie over the past two treatments and were at a loss for words.

They weren't the only ones who had come to pay their respects and remember a man who had fought to survive most of his life. My cousins were there, my brothers. Eddie's family, friends. Those we went to school with.

And I had no idea what I was going to say to these people.

I stood at the microphone staring at those in front of

me during this non-denominational service and I knew this was not *exactly* what Eddie had wanted. What he had truly wanted was to *live*. But people here, remembering him, that's what he deserved. And that's what Samantha and her family deserved.

I cleared my throat, not truly seeing those in front of me. "Eddie was my friend. He was the one who accidentally kicked a soccer ball right into a place you shouldn't kick when we were teenagers. And that one moment, when I saw stars, and I wondered exactly how I was ever going to get my low voice back again, *that moment* was when we became friends."

Laughter filled the room, and I knew I had done what I was supposed to. To make it a little lighter, to ease the burden for only a moment. Because I had tried to ease the burden before. To be the one to save the day. And I had failed. So I wouldn't fail in this.

"Eddie loved lemon pastries and chai lattes. He loved tattoos, though he never got one. So he would sit while I would get one, or Samantha, and talk about all of the art he would one day have on his skin." I cleared my throat. "But a needle never touched him. Mostly because he said every time he thought of needles, he thought of something else. So he hadn't been ready. He had been waiting." I cleared my throat again, my voice growing thick. "And I had been waiting to do my next tattoo for him. And myself. And so maybe something I should have learned long ago was *not* to wait."

I looked up at Claire in that instant, at the tears falling down her cheeks, and let out a breath. I pulled my gaze from her because I couldn't look at her when I said this. I didn't want her to be my strength. I couldn't put so much onto her, when whatever we had was so fragile, so new.

"Eddie was my friend. And when any one of us needed something, he would step in. He gave everything he could. Even when he didn't have much left some days. And the one thing he always told me he wanted to give more of, but he knew somewhere deep down that he didn't have much left—was *time*. He gave his *time* to us. However short it was by this cruel trick of fate, he gave us himself—and his time. And whatever lessons can be learned from something so devastating, is that we need to treasure those moments. Time hits you like a bullet train: it hits you fast and slides through your fingers before you have a moment to breathe. *Eddie was my friend*," I repeated. "He was joyous. He was powerful. And he ran out of time. And I am going to hate the concept and reality of that until the end of my days. But I'll always remember the time we had."

And with that, I cleared my throat again, and made my way back to sit next to Claire. She leaned her head against my shoulder, crying in deep sobs. I handed her a tissue, as everyone else began to whisper through jagged breaths and Samantha went up to speak again.

She wasn't crying, however. She had that shell-shocked look about her, that look of someone who didn't really understand how this was reality. I could truly understand that feeling. Eddie had been turning around. He was supposed to live. It was only supposed to be one little procedure.

One more thing until he could go home.

And it had killed him.

By the time she was finished speaking, telling jokes for all of our sakes so we could laugh with her, I was ready to get out of the suit, and to just get home. When we finished with the service and headed toward a restaurant to eat, my family and I didn't stay long. Everyone else had stories about his childhood and wanted to laugh, and I didn't feel like it was my place to stay.

I had tried to give him part of me, my actual literal cells, and yet those were gone. It hadn't worked again.

And I wasn't sure I could stay and watch the outcome.

So I said my goodbyes, made sure that Samantha and the rest of their family, including Eddie's grandfather, knew I was here if they needed me, but I knew they wouldn't ask. They had taken what they needed from me before, what I had freely given, and it hadn't worked. It hadn't been enough.

"Come to the house, baby," my mom said, as she cupped my cheeks.

"I just want to go home."

"No."

I looked down at her, confused. I hadn't heard that biting tone of strength in a long time. Mostly it was only when I was in trouble.

"Mom. I'm an adult."

"And you're still my baby, Kingston Montgomery. Just like Logan and Oliver are. You're going to get in that car, you're going to have Claire drive you, and you're going to come home. You're going to come home to your family and we're going to have tea, or beer, whatever you need. But you are not going to your home alone. And I'm sure that you and Claire can also be there for each other, but I'm going to be the mean mom and make you come home so I can watch you. Just for a little bit. Let me be selfish."

I knew this wasn't for her. This was for me. She was saying she could be selfish so I would blame her if I got angry. Because she was good at knowing what I needed even though I didn't want it.

"I could get angry, you know," I muttered.

"You won't. Because you want to come over too. I made pie."

I smiled at that, surprising myself that I could smile, and I went over to Claire's side. "Mom wants us to go over there. She said both of us," I warned.

"Your dad already warned me. Are you sure it's okay? I mean, I know your family because I'm friends with your family, but I don't want things to get complicated for you."

I pulled her close to me in a hug and sighed. "We sort of blew through those barn doors already. No use trying to close them."

"Lovely imagery but true. But okay, let's go get pie."

"Mom makes a damn good pie."

We ended up at my parents' home soon after. It wasn't the home we grew up in, as once the kids had moved out, they had decided to find a place a little farther out near the mountains, and where they wouldn't have to worry too much about getting kids to school and all of the events and sports that we had.

Though, ever the artist my father was, Lincoln had made sure to take out the door frame that had our heights on them and made an art piece from it that lay in Mom's library. And then of course, one of my uncles who happened to build houses for a living, had built a new door frame.

"This piece is amazing," Claire whispered under her breath as she stared at one of my dad's latest creations currently taking space in the living room.

I smiled down at her. "It really is."

"You don't take it for granted who your parents are?"

I shrugged. "They're Mom and Dads. I think what I really took for granted was the fact that I grew up in a family with two dads and a mom. Who all loved each other. Who had one bedroom, and an extra-large custom-made king." I paused and looked at her. "I'm not really sure where they found the person to make that mattress, but it works apparently." I paused, letting out a deep breath. "I meant that it works for the room. I'm just going to shut up right now."

Claire's eyes filled with laughter, and she pushed at my hip. "Whoever did the metal and woodwork though, should probably talk to your cousin Noah. I'm sure that they're going to need that big of a bed."

"Oh I'm pretty sure that Noah's parents, also a throuple, already gave them the information. It probably should concern me that there's so many throuples in my family, but no, it's just life. I like that it's normal."

"Of course it's normal. It's love. Did you ever think that you would end up in one?" she asked, and I didn't hear worry in her tone, considering we were sleeping together, and spending time together—just curiosity.

I held back a laugh at her question, surprising

myself. "No, I never wanted to share." It was the honest truth and I liked the way she blushed at my words.

"I've always wanted a real painting. One that isn't a print. Maybe one day I can afford one of your dad's. Like a small one. To fit in my wallet."

"I can try to get you a discount. Though I don't really get the family discount."

"As you shouldn't. The family would go broke if we kept allowing that," Lincoln said as he came forward and squeezed my shoulder, before giving Claire a hug. "And thank you for liking my work. Sometimes I'm afraid in my old age that I'm forgetting how to work with oils."

"Really? You're going to call yourself old?" Ethan said as he came forward, two glasses of sparkling cider in hand. He handed them both to Claire and me and we took them in thanks.

"Considering we're the same age, dear, don't call us old." Ethan winked, and Lincoln just shrugged.

"It's my prerogative."

Claire smiled at their banter. "I've been to your mom's shop too. Seriously, your family's so talented."

"And I'm just a chemist," Ethan said with such a put-upon sigh, it made me smile—once again surprising myself.

"Oh yes, please tell me more, Mr. Award-winning

and grant-winning chemist about how tough your life is."

My dads bickered in humor, trying to lighten the tension in the room, and my brothers came forward, both of them flirting with Claire, and trying to keep me smiling. Only the more they tried, the more I wanted to sink into myself.

"So, Claire, I know this isn't exactly how the whole meet the parents thing works, but should I ask how long you two have been together?" my mom asked, and as Claire's eyes widened, I scowled at my mom.

"Really? Really."

"What? I haven't met a girlfriend or whatever labels we're using now. And I'm bad at this. Remember, I ran out on one wedding before. I'm really bad at relationships."

"So bad she married both of us," Lincoln said.

Claire's eyes widened. "Wait, you ran away from a wedding?"

My mom winced. "It's a long story that I will get into later. And forget I asked the question."

"Give the boy a break. But can I have a second piece of pie?" Ethan asked, as my mom bit her lip.

"I'm sorry. I'm just trying to think of things to say that won't make everything hurt, but maybe that's not the best thing to do. But know we're here, Kingston. For you. We love you."

"I know." I set down my drink and rolled my shoulders back. "I'm going to go outside for some air."

I left them standing there, abruptly, leaving Claire to the wolves. Even though my family was anything but wolves. They were kind, caring, and had always been there for me. And I couldn't even look at them right then. Because they had all tried with me. And my friend was dead.

What were you supposed to say to that?

I stood on the deck that my uncles had built, and stared off into the distance, the icy chill of winter weather hitting. There would be another snowstorm soon, as there always was. The ice and snow coming back with a vengeance.

Everything felt bleak, as if the cold meant something more than just the bite.

A gentle hand pressed against the small of my back, and I let out a breath.

"Sorry. Just needed to think."

"There's nothing to be sorry about. We're all awkward saying the wrong things because we don't know how to help you. What you said today was beautiful though. About time. I hardly even knew Eddie, and I cried for him because of your words."

I ran a fist over my chest, trying to ignore the ache. "I didn't mean to make you cry. I was trying to lighten the mood, and it turned into tears. Didn't mean to fuck up."

"You didn't fuck up, Kingston."

I turned to look at her, scowling. "Yes, I did. It wasn't enough. Don't you understand? He wouldn't have needed this second round if my bone marrow would've worked the first time. Instead the cancer came back, and I couldn't even do it right this time. I'm still on that donor list, so even if they want to come to me, I won't do it. Because nothing I have will be enough. They'll just die. They'll have hope, and then they'll die. That's what I give them. False hope. I failed him. Just like I failed you."

I wasn't shouting the words, but I bit them out with every single ounce of hatred for myself that I had. And I was putting this all on Claire, the one person who didn't need it.

"Stop."

I swallowed hard. "Claire—"

"No. Don't think you failed me. I was stabbed and almost died and yet I knew someone was coming. I might've tried to go for help, but I knew you would be there. You and Kane. I knew how to fight, even if I knew I wasn't strong enough, because I knew you would come. For Phoebe because of Kane and just because of you, Kingston. Because you fight for those you care about, and I was lucky enough to be in that orbit. And it took far too long for me to realize that. I pushed you away because I didn't realize it. But I do now. Don't blame yourself. You give everything that you have, and I trust you with everything because of that. Eddie died because of a blood clot. Because cancer is terrible, and we still haven't found a cure. But you gave him more time with his wife. You gave him the time in the first place to find her. You gave him that time that was so precious. Remember that, Kingston. You gave him time."

I cupped her cheeks, and brushed my lips against hers, before wiping her tears away. "Thank you," I whispered, as my own tears fell, and Claire held me tight.

Out of the corner of my eye, I saw my parents holding each other with my brothers on either side of my dads. And so I held out my arms, and they came to me, and we held each other, as some of us cried, and some of us stood there stoically, nothing left but grief, and gratitude for what we held.

My friend was dead, and we'd run out of that time. Only Claire was in my arms, and something shifted.

And I had no idea what.

10

CLAIRE

"Are you sure it's okay that I'm here? I don't want to interrupt time with your boyfriend," Livvy said as she sing-songed the word *boyfriend*.

I rolled my eyes as I parked in between the lines, holding my breath as I did. I hated parking my car. It didn't matter that there were cameras all over the thing, and it could park itself if I pressed a button, it was still scary.

"He's not my boyfriend. He's well...I don't have a title or a label, and we're not going to do that. Labels are scary."

"Tell me about it. I'm sorry for even daring to tease you about it. Although he is my cousin, so I enjoy it a little bit."

"You know, I could walk down the street and bump into a cousin of yours. It oddly confused me when I found out that you were a Montgomery as well."

Livvy grinned as she got out of the car, and I followed.

"I know right? We're just all over the place. Seriously though, is it going to be too much? I know it's hard for you to get alone time with both of your jobs."

I shook my head, reached out for her hand.

"No, it's fine. We're not going to be alone here either. Crew's working out, so you'll be fine."

"And there's Aria, so it's us three girls against those two guys, we can totally kick their ass."

"Did I hear kicking ass?" Aria asked, as she hugged us both, and reached out for Livvy's phone.

"Let me see. Give, give, give."

"I already texted you with the latest photos I have of your dear baby niece."

I didn't quite understand the Montgomery family tree. Because technically Livvy was the daughter of Shep and Shea Montgomery. Meaning Livvy was a first cousin to Kane, and maybe a second cousin to Kingston and Aria who were in fact second cousins themselves. But as everybody had been raised together, and spent so much time with one another, they went by cousins no matter the connection within their generation. And to make things even more complicated, they started calling all of their kids nieces and nephews and little niblings, that way they didn't have to deal with even more cousins. So Livvy's baby girl Amelia was everyone's niece, just like Sebastian's Nora was a niece, and Luke and Landon, Leif and Brooke's sons, were nephews. I was pretty sure there were a few more kids, or there was at least going to be since I knew of two pregnancies in the generation. But they weren't even my family, so I wasn't sure how I was supposed to know everybody without name tags. Either way, them going by generation helped me tremendously.

"You know I can't get enough photos. Did you see the latest photo of Nora?" Aria asked, speaking of her actual niece. As she was a little twin to Sebastian, Sebastian's daughter was her niece by blood. However, I didn't really think titles mattered just then.

Which led me back to Kingston. And the fact that yes, we had something. Something important. But I wasn't going to call him my boyfriend. Or lover. He was just Kingston. And that was good enough for me.

And why was I suddenly all stressed out?

"She's seriously adorable. I love my niece. Any news?" Aria asked and my gaze shot up to Livvy.

Livvy pressed her lips together in a thin line and shook her head.

"No news. But it's fine. We can't find him to sign over parental rights, and the private detective and the authorities are working on it. But he ran out so quickly that he covered all paths behind him. I just hate the fact that I thought I loved him."

Aria winced. "You sometimes can't help who you fall in love with. Even if it's toxic for you."

My gaze shot to Aria, but she didn't continue, and looked relieved when both Crew and Kingston showed up, pulling into the parking lot.

"Hey there," Kingston said, as he put his arm around my waist and kissed me softly.

That answered that burning question. I guess we were truly not hiding who we were to each other. Whatever that was.

"Hi," I said, ducking my head, my cheeks blushing. For somebody who could talk dirty right back to Kingston, I was sure blushing a lot in front of him in public.

"Hold on, I need my phone. Where's my phone," Aria said, as Crew sighed.

"So nosy." Then I heard the click of a shutter on his phone and laughed over at him.

"You purposely took your phone off of silent in order to do that, didn't you?" I asked.

"Of course I did. Now smile. This is going in the family newsletter."

"You're not even a Montgomery," Livvy put in.

"No, but I figured I can send it to one of the

numerous group chats I have with you lot, and it'll all work out in the end."

"It's actually a little frightening how many Montgomery group chats you end up in," I said to my ally in this Montgomery group.

Crew just gave that bright smile of his and winked. "You don't know the half of it. Come on, non-Montgomery darling. Save me."

Kingston's hold on my hips tightened. "I don't think so, Crew. Go take your pick with one of my cousins."

"Did you just sell us off to Crew so that you could make out with your girlfriend in private?" Aria asked.

"Damn straight."

I met Livvy's gaze, as she gave me a discreet thumbs up.

It seemed the title question was now settled considering he hadn't balked at the word girlfriend.

How the hell had that happened?

"As lovely as this is, I can't leave Amelia with my mom for too long. Not that my mom isn't amazing," she said quickly, hands up. "But mostly she's a lot for a three-year-old. And I miss her." She shook her head. "Why do I always have mom guilt?"

Aria shook her head. "My mom said it was because it comes ingrained. Sorry, she still gets mom guilts. And the four of us are grown."

Livvy winced. "I still can't believe your mom had

four of you. With just me and John the house was loud enough."

Kingston cleared his throat. "At least it was you guys sprinkled in with girls, we were three boys. We were loud as hell."

I gave him a look, then steered my gaze over to Aria and Livvy, as we burst out laughing. "Oh yes, because girls are so quiet and calm and totally little princesses. Never a hair out of place."

"I feel as though I've fallen into a trap," Kingston said softly.

"Oh, you're already sunk. But it's okay, I'm still not going to save you. However, Livvy's, right. Someone's booked the gym after us, because apparently, we like to make money in this business. So let's go."

"Does he own this place?" I asked, curious.

Kingston shrugged. "I have no idea. He likes to be mysterious."

Crew smirked. "Keeps me in chicks."

"Oh yes, let me fall at your feet. Woe is me without thy charm."

"You know it," Crew said as he wrapped his arm around Aria's shoulder, and she pushed him away laughing.

Livvy just shook her head, walking on his other side, and I grinned.

I leaned toward Kingston, keeping my voice low.

"Crew used to date Daisy, right? That's how he entered into this whole family group?"

"I don't know if he dated Daisy or became best friends with Lexington first. He just showed up one day and never left." I laughed and Kingston winked. "He's one of us now. And no, he's never going to date a Montgomery again. He's been quite clear on that."

"How did you know that's what I was thinking?" I asked, liking the way that he slid his hand over mine, his thumb running circles over my palm.

"It's because I was thinking it too. The thing is," he said, his voice low, as the three of them went into their part of the gym, and we waited to enter, "Livvy is still hurting over her ex. I want to murder the man, but she won't let us look for him."

My eyes widened. "What? I thought she had a private investigator." I didn't know the whole story with Amelia's father, Livvy's ex, but I knew the relationship hadn't ended well.

"She does. Not a family member. I don't know why, that's on her. I'm pretty sure Noah knows where the asshole is or could type a few clicks on his fancy keyboard and find him. But he hasn't yet because Livvy asked him not to. Because she wants to do this on her own, and not rely on him. If Amelia was ever in danger though, or if we needed the man right away? I'm sure she'd come to us. Because that's what family does."

"I sort of get her point. Not wanting to be a burden."

"Livvy is never a burden. Neither are you. But back to our point, I don't see her and Crew together."

"What about Aria?" I teased.

"Aria is in love with someone else," he whispered, his voice low.

There was only one man I could think of that turned Aria into knots—something no one really voiced aloud. "Travis?" I asked, speaking of Aria's friend who I didn't know well. In fact, I'd only met him a few times. He was the life of the party, but not always around for her. But I didn't know him well enough to know if he was good for Aria or not. Nor did I know his feelings about her.

"You got it in one."

"I've only met him a few times, and I wasn't really a fan. Does that make me a bad person?"

Kingston snorted. "Not at all. I hate him. He was supposed to come up to that cabin, and while I'm forever grateful for that snowstorm because it was just you and me in the end, I'm doubly grateful that he wasn't there. It makes me the annoying big brother asshole, but I can't stand him."

"There's just something about him…"

"Yep. And Aria might see it, because she's brilliant,

but she's either ignoring it, or thinking she can fix him."

"You can never fix them."

His brow raised and I shrugged.

"I could have had stupid boyfriends in high school and college. Not mean ones, just stupid ones."

"Well, I'll try not to be a stupid one."

My lips twitched, and then he leaned down and pressed his mouth to mine.

"Come on, let's go on the next phase of self-defense before we have to deal with actual work."

"True, I'm overloaded at work right now, but my assistant Trix is on it today."

"I would think this time of year would be the hardest for you."

"So much so. Though wedding season in the spring isn't much better. But I don't mind it. Long hours mean I'm rarely home, and if I am home, I'm working, and that's not really a great thing to say to the guy that you're sleeping with."

"I'm working long hours too. Those big parties? They need security. But we'll find time. Don't worry, and by the way, is it okay that I didn't correct her when she said girlfriend?"

I stared up at him. "Stop reading my mind."

"What? I have no idea what the hell I'm doing."

"Okay good. We don't know what the hell we're doing together. That's a good label."

"Sure. I'm pretty simple though."

"You're anything but simple, Kingston Montgomery."

"True. But I don't mind."

———

BY THE TIME we were done with training, I was sweaty, a little sore, and my phone was blowing up with work things.

Crew ended up driving Aria and Livvy back to their houses since he was heading that way, and since Kingston had driven here with Crew, we ended up back at my place, with him driving my car so I could work on my phone the whole time.

I looked over at Kingston and winced. "I'm sorry. Things get a little busy."

"We get things done though. Now get to work."

"Aye aye, sir."

"You can call me sir anytime you want."

I flipped him off, and he leaned forward and kissed my middle finger, making both of us laugh. "Do you want to come in?" I asked as we pulled into my driveway, and he turned off the car and nodded.

"Yeah. Since we do have your car."

I pressed my phone against my forehead and groaned.

"I really did not think of the logistics of this."

"It's fine. Kane can pick me up on the way to our night job, or I can hang out here with you for a bit. Just whatever you want."

"I forgot you have to work tonight."

"Yep. But it's fine. I don't mind. I know you have work to do too."

"Let me make you something quick to eat, and we can just hang out while we do some work."

He wiggled his brows, and I rolled my eyes.

"I meant actual work. But you know, whatever."

"Naked work it is," he shouted, and I laughed, getting out of the car.

"I like your place," he said, as I closed the security down, and flipped the locks. It was so ingrained in that moment that I didn't even think about it, but I saw him notice.

Only, I had done it out of habit. Not out of fear. And not even because Kingston was here with me. I didn't think that a couple of lessons in self-defense was really going to save the day, or keep me any steadier, but maybe, just maybe, I was figuring out how to be okay.

Or maybe I was just making a big deal out of everything.

"I can make a quick pasta, some lemon and chicken. There's some defrosted in the fridge."

"That sounds good. You let me know what you need help with."

"I actually don't mind people helping me in the kitchen. Unlike some of our friends."

"They're so mean," he said with a laugh, and we ended up in my kitchen, cooking together, each of us taking breaks to look at our phones and work, and it felt natural.

Everything felt safe. And that wasn't a word I used lightly, not anymore.

"Okay, you have to tell me exactly how you made that sauce," he said as we finished our dinner, and rinsed off our plates before putting them in the dishwasher.

"I literally just added some wine and lemons and hoped for the best."

"That's how my dad Lincoln cooks, my dad Ethan is *way* more analytical."

"I wouldn't have imagined that," I said sarcastically.

"I know right? Considering his job."

"I almost want to ask how it was like living with two dads and a mom, but then I saw the way that they were with you, and it just felt right. Like you just had somebody else there in your life that loved you."

"You nailed it on the head. It was always a little

awkward at soccer games or PTA meetings. But people got used to us. And poly relationships that create families are becoming more mainstream now. There's even TV shows with those kinds of relationships that are canon."

"I know, you're so blasé now. No longer pushing the envelope."

"Don't worry, I'm pretty sure the Montgomerys will find a way to make a poly cube or something."

"I am one hundred percent sure I could not handle that. Way too many limbs."

"And I don't like to share," he whispered, before leaning down and pressing his lips to mine.

I shut the water off, and groaned, moving so he could cage me against the counter.

I should have felt worried, should have wanted to push him away. But I didn't. Instead I moaned into him, sliding my hands up the back of his shirt.

"When do you have to go to work?"

"Kane will be here in an hour," he said as he nibbled at my jaw.

"That should be enough time."

"We'll see. I still need to finish eating."

And when he went to his knees and shoved down my sweats, I groaned.

"Okay, okay," I panted, and then my panties were pulled to the side, and his mouth was on me.

I loved Kingston's tongue. He could flatten it just right to cover my entrance, before curling it right at my clit. I wasn't sure how he did those laps, and it was something I wanted to watch fully at some point. He kept going, tasting and sucking, and it took all within me not to fall into a puddle just then. And when he speared me with two fingers, no warning, I came. Just like with a trigger, I was gone, my toes curling, my hands gripping the counter.

"Kingston," I panted.

"That's it, say my name."

I smiled down at him, and his blue eyes grew darker, his tongue darting out to lick his lips. With his hand still covering me, I knelt in front of him, cupping his cheeks, and kissed him.

"You taste so fucking good," he groaned.

"I like the fact that I can taste myself on your mouth."

"You are going to like that more and more. Because I'm never going to stop."

A small part of me twisted in the best way possible, my pulse racing at his words.

Never stop. Because this could be more.

But no, I needed to push those thoughts out of my mind. This had all happened so fast, and I was just trying to catch up. So I pushed reality out of my mind and let myself just live in this moment.

With Kingston Montgomery.

The man, not the dream or the memory.

He kept kissing me, and then I was on my feet again, hands pressed to the counter. He'd shoved my shirt up, and pushed my bra up as well so my breasts were free, his large hands cupping them.

"I love the fact that they're too fucking big for my hands."

"They get in the way."

"Not for me." He plucked at my nipples, sending shivers down my spine, and I could feel the hard length of him against my back.

"I want you."

"Then take me."

I heard him reach into his pocket, the crinkle of a condom, and I was grateful. I only had them in my bedroom, and apparently, I was supposed to sprinkle them all over the house. I would. Next time.

And then he was pressing against me, and I went on my tiptoes, both of us groaning as he slid deep inside me. He held onto my hips, and then pulled out, before achingly pushing into me inch by inch.

It was hard and fast, and I could barely count my breaths before I was coming again, and he was following me.

He leaned over me, both of us sprawled over my counter, shaking.

"I don't think I've ever had sex in the kitchen before." I looked up at the cameras that I had positioned around my house for security and winced. "And I'm pretty sure that was just recorded."

He kissed the back of my neck, and then my shoulder, and smiled against me. "I'll take care of the feed. Don't worry, no one else can see. You're safe."

"I know," I whispered, knowing it for the truth.

I was safe. With him. Wasn't that a scary thought?

He pulled out of me, and I immediately felt the ache between my legs. We cleaned up, and then sanitized the kitchen, laughing together, before we went back to work. His phone buzzed again, and he frowned at the readout.

"What's wrong?"

"I don't recognize the number, but it's not spam."

He answered, his face going gray as the other person spoke. I set down my phone and moved to sit right next to him, thigh to thigh, so I could put my hand on his.

"Yes. Yes. Tomorrow works. Thank you. Yeah, no problem. I'll be there."

He ended the call, and then sat there for a full thirty seconds without speaking, his heartbeat racing from the way that his pulse beat on his neck.

"Kingston?" I whispered.

"That was the testing center. They found another match."

My eyes widened, and I turned to look at him fully. Another match for his bone marrow. I knew it was incredibly rare and almost never happened, but from what I'd read it *could*. But for it to happen so soon after losing Eddie? My heart broke, only fastened together knowing that it needed to be the strong one here for him.

"Can you donate so quickly?"

"It's been a few weeks now. So yeah. I think? They said it averages out around twenty days. I don't really know the logistics of it, but they want me to come in and do testing. Just to make sure that I can."

I held his hand, my heart racing. "Did they tell you anything else?" *And how were you feeling?*

"No. They didn't tell me anything about them or timing other than getting in for testing. It can be anonymous, or they can meet me. I don't know really what would be best. But it's up to them. Right? If they want to meet me, I'll be there. If that's what they need."

I knew I was going to probably say the wrong thing, but Kingston never thought of himself. Even if it broke me to do so. "You can protect yourself too by not knowing." Because there was no question in Kingston donating if he physically could. He'd give every ounce of himself without realizing he'd left nothing for the man in the mirror.

"No, I'll meet them. If they want. Because that's what they need."

Needs and wants. He kept using those words. But he wasn't protecting himself. He had broken because his friend had died. Because he thought he wasn't enough.

And now he was going to do it again, only a few weeks later.

Only he wouldn't do it alone. He was slowly teaching me how to find my own strength—to find my own safety.

So I'd do the same for him.

Even if I didn't know what it would mean.

11

KINGSTON

Tension on the job could kill. At least on my job. However, thanks to a team who knew what they were doing, I could at least try to lean into the chaotic thoughts that kept wrapping their way around me.

Getting the call from the hospital with Claire by my side had once again changed everything.

While part of me had wanted to jump off that couch and drive hell-bent to the hospital and do whatever I could for that person, that wasn't reality. Reality was the crushing sense of disappointment, knowing that I probably wasn't going to be able to do it.

There were so many uncertainties when it came to what happened next.

Maybe I didn't have enough bone marrow. Maybe I

wasn't fully a match. There was more to do than just a simple blood test. There were countless other things. Maybe I would get a cold. Maybe I'd be on a job and fall off a fucking ladder because of a dog and hurt myself to the point that I couldn't do it. I could freeze to death in a snowstorm, and not be able to do anything.

Or maybe I could donate, bleed and be in pain and be sore and do everything that I possibly could and fail again.

My job was to keep people safe. And I hadn't done it with Eddie.

"What's going on, Kingston? Everything okay?" Daisy asked, as she came toward me, speaking into her mic so her voice was louder in my earpiece, and we weren't disrupting the activities around me.

I shrugged, keeping my attention on the bigwig we were guarding for the afternoon. This was a last-minute setup, the local billionaire needing additional security for a charity event. Ford and Noah had done most of the setup for it, and Daisy and I were coming in to pinch hit for additional security since the man had gotten a few death threats.

Security details and bodyguard services were our normal job—this, and countless other things—and I needed to get my head in the game.

The fact that these death threats were because the man was donating hundreds of millions of dollars to different charities and organizations, flabbergasted me. The man was in the middle of depleting his estate he'd made after building a company that had developed a lifechanging scientific achievement. He'd made hundreds of millions in a few years and had become a billionaire because of it. Now he was in the midst of donating a majority of it to foundations to help others. Only not everyone was happy with how he spent it.

No, from the way that the man kept being headline news, he was going to need us again.

I pulled myself out of my thoughts on our client and focused on Daisy. "I'm fine." Not quite a lie.

"Did you get contacted yet?" my cousin asked, and I nodded.

"Prep work tomorrow. Hopefully." A few more tests and discussions. And a heartbreaking chance.

"You're a good man, Kingston."

I sighed, not feeling it so much right now. "It's a kid, Daisy. A *kid*." In the day since the call, the family of the young boy with leukemia had agreed to tell me a little more about their son in hope and appreciation. They hadn't wanted it to be anonymous and while I hadn't reached out personally, I knew that I would.

Because of Eddie.

Because of a little kid who needed me.

A little boy named Buckley.

A nine-year-old who had fought to survive for over half of his life.

And I was his last chance.

Her eyes went somber, and she reached out, squeezing my arm in reassurance. With a tight nod, we went back to work, doing my best to keep all eyes on the exits. Today was pretty quiet, not that I ever say the Q word aloud. That was just asking for an issue.

"Hey, Kingston," Ford said as he came toward me, and I tilted my head, keeping my eye on our client.

"We good?"

"We have a few more plans to deal with coming up. Depending on when you have to donate and how much time you have to take off, let us know. We have another client coming in."

I frowned, darting my attention to him for a second before going back to work. "Anyone I know from the books?"

"They're filming a huge hopeful blockbuster out in Boulder later in January, and they need to beef up security for a couple of their A-listers." He rattled off a very familiar name, and I blinked.

"Really? Doesn't she have her own team?"

"She's in between teams right now, and the studio wants to hire us. We will be stretched a bit thin because we have two other events that week, but I figured, if you're up for it."

"It depends on the hospital I guess." I winked. "I hate not knowing."

"I understand. We've got Hugh there too, and a couple of our backups. So don't worry, we'll handle it. But I want you on point if you can."

"No problem. And if I can't?"

"Then Hugh can do it. He's good," he said, speaking of our British hire, who happened to be in love with Daisy.

"Sounds good. What time does this wrap up again?"

"In about ten minutes. You're off if you want. We've got the rest of this. I know you have family dinner tonight."

I snorted. "I swear, how do you know all these things?"

"Noah knew it. I'm just lucky that my husband keeps a spreadsheet." Ford beamed as he said *husband,* and I just smiled at the man, before checking out and making sure that everything was set for my leaving.

I liked this job. I liked doing what I could to make sure that things just made sense rationally. I liked the adrenaline, and the puzzle solving. I didn't like the fact that I felt as if I were on the outside looking in a bit more than I used to. Which wasn't like me.

With an odd sigh, I said goodbye to the others and got in my car. As it had only been an afternoon event, it meant I still had dinner with my family which I was grateful for. We didn't get to do core family dinners often. In fact, we would still have at least one straggler, if not more, for dinner. But the core group would be there. My two brothers and my three parents. I had a feeling Livvy would be there too, since she had been helping my mom with something at the shop earlier that morning, and that meant Mom would give Livvy an invite. And that meant her daughter Amelia would be there, and I loved that kid. She was fricking adorable.

Claire was working at an event tonight and would be working non-stop until a few of her events settled down. She worked longer hours than I did sometimes, and that was saying something. And it was odd to think that Claire would come to mind so easily. She'd always been on the periphery, a friend of a friend, but now she was someone I thought of first. I wasn't sure what to make of that.

Feelings were a tricky thing. How did I feel about Claire?

I didn't know. I wanted her. I liked her. I craved her.

But beyond that?

What did we want?

Hell. That was too much to think about right now so I wouldn't. Claire and I were fine. We just...*were*.

I pulled into my parents' driveway as they'd left a spot for me. There was usually enough street parking, but it seemed that another neighbor was having people over that night, so they had left me space. It was just those little things, but that showed they were always thinking about me. Always thinking about all of us.

I looked down at my work suit, and figured maybe I should have changed, but I could fit into my dad Lincoln's clothes if I wanted to get comfortable. I hadn't brought a change of clothes because I hadn't been thinking. No, I had been more worried about making sure that I had everything in the car for dinner.

I got out and went to the backseat to pull out a dried fruit and nut tray thing that I had gotten at the store, as well as a couple of loaves of bread that hopefully were fine. It wasn't the greatest thing for dinner, but it could stay in the car when I was at work. I hadn't been sure when I was going to get off, because it depended on the client, and I was glad Ford had at least let me out a little bit early.

The door opened, and Ethan walked out, a wide grin on his face. "You're here. We thought you'd be late."

Hands full, I just shrugged. "I got lucky. Working with family has its perks."

My dad moved forward and took one of the bags from my hands. "You didn't have to bring anything you know. You know we always cook for an army."

"We *are* an army. We need all the food. And I need some protein." At the sound of a gleeful shout, I looked up. Amelia bounced in the doorway, and I grinned over at her.

"Hey there, baby Amelia." My niece was freaking delightful. Livvy had put her in pigtails and a winter dress with tights and she looked like a little princess.

"Uncle Kingston! Mommy and I are here for dinner! I love dinner!"

"Me too, babe." My dad chuckled beside me as we moved toward the house, watching Amelia bounce on her toes since she was clearly not allowed out of the doorway—smart kid.

"Amelia, darling, away from the door, please." Livvy's voice rang out, she ran forward, her long hair flowing down her back, and she picked up her daughter, and set her on her hip. She was getting so big that it surprised me that Livvy could pick her up so easily with how slender she was, but all moms were strong. I had learned that firsthand.

"It's okay, I'm here, and I've got nuts."

"Nuts. Nuts!" Amelia said repeatedly, clapping her little hands together, and my dad groaned while Livvy just glared at me.

I gave the most innocent smile ever, before I leaned down, blew a raspberry on Amelia's cheek, and then did the same to Livvy just to make her laugh.

My cousin just rolled her eyes at me and then kissed

my cheek. "Thanks for that," she said, sarcasm dripping from her voice.

"Nuts. Kiss. Nuts. Kiss."

Amelia could speak in full sentences, and was a little rock star, but sometimes she just liked to scream one word at me, mostly because she enjoyed seeing her mom roll her eyes at the whole screaming bad words thing.

As expected, both of my brothers, Oliver and Logan were there, as was my cousin Lake. I frowned at one of the co-owners of Montgomery Ink Legacy and Montgomery Security, and she just smiled wide at me.

"I heard there was food. I couldn't help but want to be here."

I opened my arms, and my cousin hugged me tightly. She had been through so much during the last few years, and I couldn't help but hold her a bit tighter. Even though she was happily married, and a mother to a very beautiful little girl, I couldn't help but remember the same Lake who had stared at me with wide eyes, and dark circles under her eye with dark circles underneath those, begging us for help.

She seemed to sense what I was thinking and tapped me on the chin. "Stop worrying about me, Kingston. I'm doing fantastic. I love Nick—he's an amazing husband who loves me. And I have a beautiful daughter who makes every day worth living beyond any measure. I'm not in that place anymore. We have other family members to worry about." She lifted a brow and I sighed.

"Yeah, yeah."

"Hey, you brought nuts," Oliver said, shaking the bag I'd brought.

Livvy groaned. "Seriously?"

My brother blinked innocently. "What? I like nuts."

"I'm not going to say anything to that," Logan said wisely, as my other dad came into the room, a tray of drinks and hand.

"Especially not in this house," Lincoln said, and I pinched the bridge of my nose, as Livvy just gave up, and laughed as Amelia began to ask what was so funny.

This was family. Yes, it was our core group, with a couple of stragglers, but that's what family was. I had eaten at Kane's family's house often, just as the same as I had at Lex's. We had all grown up as siblings, and it made sense that as long as we were all accounted for, we had a place to sleep and eat at night.

With the next generation in, such as Lake's daughter and Livvy's, it was going to be even more so. And that there was a crib upstairs as well as a child's bed just in case some random grandchild that wasn't even theirs decided to come by, made me smile.

"This is incredible," Oliver said as he rubbed his

stomach as if he were a toddler. Amelia decided to mimic him, and the table erupted in laughter.

"Your dad made the brisket, I made the potatoes, and Ethan made the rest," my mom said, looking pleased with herself.

Ethan smiled. "And you didn't burn the potatoes."

"I'm a good cook."

"Just not with mashed potatoes."

My mom sighed dramatically, reaching over to tickle Amelia at the same time. "I let it burn one time because I was trying to help Kingston get his hand out of his pants, and here we go."

Livvy and Lake both choked on their drinks, as Amelia looked on in confusion.

"I was three, and I had just realized that if I played with my penis, it was fun. I'm very sorry."

"What's a penis?" Amelia asked.

"Sorry." I ducked my head at Livvy's glare, a smile playing on my face.

"Well, you haven't really grown out of that newfound love of doing that, have you?" Oliver asked.

"But now he has someone else to help him with that," Logan said with a grin, and I glared at both of them.

"Okay, it is time for cleanup," Livvy said, as she plucked a now red-faced and giggling Amelia out of her booster. "You guys talk about whatever you need to, and we're going to protect little ears."

"I'll go with you," Lake said with a laugh. "Nick is on baby duty tonight, and I want to call before I head home, because I miss them."

"I never asked, why were you up in Boulder?" I pulled on her sleeve slightly, smiling down at her.

"I had a meeting downtown, and instead of driving the hour and a half back through traffic, your parents told me I had to eat dinner here and drive later once rush hour was over. Well, your mom did. It was an order."

"Yes, it was," my mom said with a grin.

"And I don't mind it, Nick and Harlow need some bonding time without me hovering. Because I hover."

"Only the best moms do," Livvy said, as the two went upstairs, and my mother looked on with a happy smile.

Then she turned her attention back to us. "I need grandkids. I know I'm way too young to be a grand-mother, but please make me one."

I held back a laugh, knowing she was only partly kidding. My parents didn't pressure. Ever.

"I will do my best," Oliver said, and she threw a roll at her youngest son. I laughed as Oliver caught it with his mouth, threw both hands in the air, and cheered as Logan clapped.

"I swear to God," Lincoln said as he pinched the bridge of his nose.

"You are all ridiculous. But I love you," my mom said.

"As for the grandkid, how are things with Claire?" Ethan asked, and I just shook my head.

"I swear, you guys were a little more subtle when we were teenagers and trying to have the sex talk."

"We were better at the sex," Lincoln said, "because we were really good at having sex."

"Yes, we are. I mean, if any one of the sets of the Montgomerys are going to be good about having the talk, it's going to be one of the triads. I'm just saying."

Both of my brothers closed their eyes, and covered their ears, while I just laughed. I was used to their antics. We had always been open and honest about sex and growing up. I lived in an unconventional household in some respects, so that meant we had had a lot of questions when we were younger. More like why we had three parents and some people only had two. And all three of my parents had decided if they hid anything, it would make things worse for us. And they were always open about wanting to make sure we were open with them. Meaning as soon as I got my first girlfriend when I was fourteen, my dad sat down, and explained that while sex was fun, I should wait until I was older. Because emotions always came through it, even if you wanted to pretend there weren't any. And then he had handed me a pack of condoms and said if I was going to be dumb and work with just my hormones, I needed to remember my brain just a little bit.

I hadn't needed those condoms for a couple of more years, but I had been grateful for the new pack that he had given me because the first one had been expired.

That was my family, always taking care of us—only that meant they were always nosy.

My mom smiled. "I'm just saying, Claire seems really nice. I'm so glad that we got to meet her at that event."

I shook my head. "You've known Claire for a while now. She's Phoebe's best friend."

"And Phoebe and Kane are adorable. I know they're living together now. Do you know if Kane's planning on asking Phoebe to marry him?" My mom held up both hands. "I'm not saying that they have to be married to live together. Hello, that is not who we are."

"I know, I know," I said with a laugh. "I think Phoebe's working on figuring out her new family situation, you know, with the whole secret family thing."

Phoebe, it turned out, had a whole set of siblings that nobody else had known about, so she was dealing with the consequences of that and trying to get to know them. It wasn't always smooth sailing, but I knew my cousin was taking care of her.

"That's true. I don't know, I just like weddings. And with so many cousins, that means we get to have a lot of them. Doesn't Claire plan weddings and receptions?"

"I love how you circled back, and she does some. She likes doing all types of events, and not just weddings."

"Well, speaking of events..." Mom began, and I was grateful for the change of subject, at least I thought I would be. "The Montgomery family party might have to be canceled."

"Why?" Logan asked. "It's seriously my favorite part of the year."

We didn't always have a multi-family holiday party in the Montgomery household, but there was always at least one major event where every Montgomery was invited. This year it was post-holiday season and things got tricky time wise. That meant a lot of bodies in one place, and a lot of planning. Every set the four main branches hosts on a rotating schedule. They did the same for the family reunions that we had. This year, it was the Boulder family, with my grandpa and grandma in charge, and that meant my parents were helping plan the most since it was their turn. It was very compli-cated, and there was a spreadsheet involved, because of course there was a spreadsheet involved. And I knew that one day soon, it would be our job to deal with that.

But for now, I just let them deal with the planning. Or at least I thought I did.

Oliver leaned forward. "What's going on?"

Mom's face darkened and both of my dads reached out to pat her hands. "The place that we usually have it at when in Boulder canceled on us."

"The lodge? Why the hell would they cancel on us?" I asked.

"Because they're bastards. They wanted triple the money because they had another event double booked, and they canceled on us. We'll figure it out," Lincoln said, with a sigh. "But I don't think we're going to be able to work with all of the little pieces as well as we usually do. It's going to be a little more hectic, considering all of us are in some of our busiest seasons."

Mom pressed both hands together in front of her. "I know Claire is horribly busy, but do you think she could help?"

I narrowed my gaze, trying to see exactly where I had gone wrong here.

"Are you serious right now, Mom?"

Mom held up both hands, looking very innocent. "I swear, I just need help planning because every single other person in our family right now is doing a thousand things. I just want us to have a lovely event like we always do. But I know Claire is in her busiest season, so ignore me. And just because she happens to be your girlfriend or whatever label that you're using, doesn't mean that I'm really needling. Maybe."

"I really don't believe anything about that innocent tone."

"There's nothing innocent about your mother," Ethan said as he sipped his drink, and Lincoln snorted, while my mother just glared at them both.

"I'll deal with you two later."

"And that's our cue to go," Logan said with a laugh as both Livvy and Lake came down, Amelia dancing between them.

"I'll text her and see. But she'll probably be too busy."

"I know. And we'd pay her. I don't want her to think we're taking advantage. Because Montgomerys don't do that. We always pay our way."

Lake squeezed my shoulder as she walked by. "Oh, you thought of using Claire for the event. That's good. If Claire can't come, I have a backup, But we should use Claire. Keep it in the family."

"Et tu, Brute, Lake?" I asked.

Lake looked so innocent, but I knew there was nothing of the sort. "I don't know what you're talking about."

As we went to clean up the table, Mom shoved me into the living room, and I held out both hands. "I'll ask. I'll ask."

"I know it's a big ask. And frankly, I know that Claire will probably be too busy to help. We Montgomerys can handle most things, but I also know that Claire needs things to focus on." She bit her lip and I frowned.

"What do you mean?"

"She's just like you and your brothers from what I've seen. I know she went through so much and I'm grateful that she's doing better, but Phoebe said she's been pushing herself and her business since. Maybe I'm reading too much into it."

I squeezed her hand, the memory of Claire on the floor slamming into me. "She's making a name for herself for sure. I don't like remembering her like that, Mom."

Mom cupped my cheeks with both hands. "She's safe. She's healthy. And she has you. Though I do hate that you work in a job that puts you in danger."

"Mom…"

"No, no, I'll stop. You're good at what you do. I just get worried. Now, about the event…"

I exhaled and wrapped my arms around her. She had always been bigger than life, but now her head barely came up to my shoulders. "I'll take care of it."

"I love you. And if it's too weird, because I know you guys are just starting out on your relationship, don't worry about it. I swear I'm not trying to be weird about it."

"I love you. Meddler."

She kissed my cheek, and then went off to the rest of the family, as I looked down at my phone.

ME:

> Hey, it turns out that my mom might need help finishing with the planning of the Montgomery Family Event. All caps.

I quickly tried to explain everything that had occurred, and then sighed.

ME:

> I know that it's probably too late, but if you have any spare time to help with a spreadsheet or an idea or something, I think they're finding a venue, but they could use your help. Or my mom's meddling. I don't know.

CLAIRE:

> Yes. I'm in. I love Montgomery parties. And I just had a cancellation. Mostly because the engagement is over, and now I'm out their fees.

ME:

> Well, shit. My mom said she'd pay you.

ME:

> If that's weird...

CLAIRE:

Business with friends is always weird, but I can work something out. Haha. Honestly, with a cancellation, I could use the money, but I'll talk to your mom about that. I don't want to take advantage.

ME:

That's exactly what she said.

I sighed, then continued.

ME:

But you do realize that you'll be working directly with my mother and that means she is going to be sitting down and wanting to get to know you.

CLAIRE:

I figured. But oh.

ME:

Oh.

CLAIRE:

I'm still in.

ME:

Good. I'll let her get a hold of you. You doing okay?

CLAIRE:

I am. I have to get back to work. But I'll talk to you tonight? We still have to finish that movie.

We were watching a movie over the phone, since both of us were a little busy right now, and it felt weird, and yet not.

ME:

Game on. Talk to you soon.

CLAIRE:

You too.

I put my phone in my pocket, then headed back into the room with my family. Things were a little out of control, overlapping and making me feel as if it was all too much, but as the snow began to fall, just a little bit and it would still be safe to drive, I listened to my family laugh, and clean up. The doctors would call soon, and I would find that path.

And I would end the night on the phone with Claire. Again.

12

CLAIRE

I woke drenched in sweat, odd whispers in my mind as I tried to pull myself into reality and out of my terror dreams once again. I took a deep breath, and then another. I would be fine. I had to be fine.

"It's just a dream. It's just a dream."

I continued to repeat that phrase to myself, the blood pounding in my ears finally dissipating so I could hear my alarm going off.

I reached over and pressed a button on my phone to stop it, and then ran my hands over my face again. At least the dream had come right before my alarm, so I wasn't up at three o'clock in the morning again, screaming.

I didn't have as many nightmares as I usually had. I

didn't know if it was because therapy was working, time had moved on, or maybe because I could rely on someone.

Although Kingston wasn't in bed beside me. He had gone to his family dinner the night before, and we had talked late into the night for hours over the phone, each of us having early morning appointments and meetings. We didn't spend every hour together, but I did think about him more often than not. Perhaps that should worry me, or perhaps it just meant that this was normal. What did I know? I hadn't been in a serious relationship in a long time. And even then, this felt different. Probably because we had been friends first, and the trauma that had brought us together still ebbed within my nightmares as was evident this morning.

I had only had that one nightmare with Kingston at my side, and I didn't know what to make of that. In the few times he had slept over since, I hadn't had a dream where I'd woken up in a cold sweat and panic. I had dreamt peacefully, and woke up in his arms, naked, and warm.

I was fine without him being here. I didn't want to have to rely on him being beside me to be okay. And I didn't want to rely on the idea of a man to protect me, or him in my life forever. It was way too early for that, and although I had had a crush on him for as long as I had known him, things were different now. He was different.

And I was beyond crushing on the man. I had learned who he truly was.

I didn't want to rely on that, I told myself again, so I got out of bed, and told myself I would go through my day, and I would talk to him later. It was girls' night, something I didn't get to do often, but we were trying to be more social even during our busy season, and then afterward, I would talk with Kingston. Because he was mine. If only for a little while.

I took a quick shower and got ready for my day, going through my list on my phone and everything else that I had to work through.

I didn't have any events today, as I only had planning meetings and phone calls galore. And I was grateful for that. Meaning I didn't need to wear an outfit to fit another event. I could wear leggings and a cute top, and that would work for the girls' night as well. I quickly put on my makeup, and then sent myself a voice text to make sure that I had everything set up when I got to my office.

I headed to my office, still surprised that I even had one. When I had first started my business, I had worked out of my home. It had just made sense and was better for cost saving. And then I had started to need to meet clients face to face, rather than at a coffee shop, or at the venue.

Now I felt like I was a grown-up, with a real place of business, and things working out.

Of course, I knew if I said that out loud, things would probably blow up in my face, so it was best to keep things in my mind.

I was excited to start working on the Montgomery event. I knew that it was usually a well-oiled machine because they had so many years of practice, but with the new venue, and the late notice of some things, Kingston's mom was in a panic. But I was working with her and would do my best to help. The fact that I had had a cancellation at all irked me and made me feel horrible for the couple, but maybe it was a good omen. Because I got to work with the Montgomerys. And they always did a fantastic party. While part of me wondered if this was just a pity thing, the other part of me knew that everyone else had full-time jobs, and they wanted to be able to relax.

So I would help them have the best party ever. Because while I wasn't a Montgomery, I was one of their friends, so that meant I had been trapped in the spiderweb long ago.

By the time I finished working on that with Holland, and a couple of Kingston's aunts and uncles, I was hyped up for the event, and ate lunch while working on a retirement party set for a couple of months from now. We were just in the initial steps, but this one was going to have at least three hundred people there. It touched me that the woman retiring had so many people connected to her who wanted to celebrate the life she had led and the people that she had helped. So I would do my best to showcase her career. And make sure she knew that this wasn't the end. But a new beginning.

I smiled at that and wiggled in my seat as I continued to work. I loved my job. I loved events that just made sense and clicked. I loved the dogs' birthdays and the weddings and small birthday parties for two. Because yes, sometimes I planned those, so it was a surprise and intimate for the other person involved.

I loved what I did. And it did make me feel like I had another feather in my cap because I was working on a Montgomery party.

I just didn't want to think too hard about that.

By the time I was done, I had been working for far too long, since I had been up since four o'clock. But I had more on my list to do before my girls' night. So I packed things up, and continued calls in the car before I went to the grocery store to pick up my order. Thankfully, the shopper there seemed to understand what a ripe fruit and not moldy vegetable was, so everything looked good in the bags, and I headed over to my brother's house.

My brother lived in a small two-bedroom home on the other side of the suburb from me, and it was still a work in progress. Hudson had spent most of their savings on his wife's cancer treatments, and it broke me to think even with insurance, it hadn't been enough. And so now Hudson was starting over, not just in life, but with savings and a new job, and figuring out how to be a single dad.

I was so damn proud of him, and even though he was the older brother, I did all I could to take care of him.

Case in point, me showing up with groceries. He answered the door, a scowl on his face, as I looked around for the kids.

"Are they with Mom and Dad?"

"Yes, they're having grandparent day. It's so good to see you. Hello. Why are you here with groceries, little sister?"

I smiled brightly and danced on my toes. "I'm here because I love you."

"I'm supposed to be the one who takes care of you," my big brother said with a scowl before he kissed the top of my head and took the bags from me.

"You do take care of me. All the time. But I know you worked a double, so I wanted to pick up groceries."

Hudson exhaled and took the bags from me, letting me inside the house. "I know how much you make a year, Claire. You can't afford to take care of my groceries and your own. The Montgomerys pay me well. And I make a very respectable living doing what I do. It's not always an option for someone to be a full-time tattoo artist and take care of their kids. But I'm working on it. Having childcare taken care of is a huge help."

"Most of the Montgomerys have kids now, at least the ones that work with you. So it makes sense they'd have it taken care of."

Hudson shrugged, putting everything away with the ease of a man who knew his home and was finally comfortable in it. "And apparently their parents did the same thing. So I'm using it, because it came with the job, and that way I don't feel guilt."

I shook my head, studying my brother's face. "Like you feel guilt for me bringing groceries? But didn't you bring me groceries two weeks ago?"

"Of course I did. Because you're my baby sister." He leaned down and kissed my forehead so of course I blew a raspberry at him.

"And you're my big brother. So get over it. I love you. Jerk."

"We're all so cute making sure that we keep the pet names going. Speaking of pet names...does Kingston call you by something? Or is it something that I'm going to have to kick his ass for?"

"That is the least subtle I've ever heard you in my life."

"We know I'm not good at that shit. Seriously though, is he taking good care of you? Do I need to kick his ass?"

"You don't get to kick my boyfriend's ass."

"So he's your boyfriend now."

I rolled my eyes. "Maybe? Someone called me his girlfriend in front of him and he agreed with it." Hudson just rolled his eyes even as my stomach tightened. "It's good to know that hasn't changed over the years."

"I like the Montgomerys, Claire. I do. And I like Kingston. But I know you've had a crush on him for a while."

I blushed, frowning at him. "How did you know?"

"Like I said. I'm your brother. It's what we do. Does he know?"

"That I had a crush on him when he didn't even see me? Yes. It was awkward as hell, and I sort of just blurted it out."

He snorted. "That sounds about right."

"I don't know what I'm doing, other than I think I'm happy. Which is scary."

"It's scary to be happy?" he asked softly.

"I think you of all people know better than to be confused about asking that."

"You're right. I just don't want you to get hurt."

"Why do you think I would get hurt?"

"I'm not saying you will. I'm just saying that I don't know, I just don't like the idea of me working with the family of the guy that you're seeing, and you being friends with a lot of them. All of our webs are a little too tangled."

I rolled my eyes, even though he was hitting on a point I tried not to think about. "Stop worrying. Worrying is for me to do."

He reached out and tapped the side of my face, and I frowned, putting my hand up to his.

"What is it?"

"I see the dark circles your concealer's not hiding. Don't you have that color corrective shit?"

I pulled away, embarrassed. "Trust the tattoo artist to know about that. And thank you for making me feel like crap."

"Nightmares?"

I couldn't lie to him, not when he could see the evidence stamped on my face. "Yes, a nightmare. But I'm getting better. And I'm talking to my therapist."

"I'm glad to hear about the therapist, not so glad about the nightmares. And I'm sorry for making you frown and think too hard about Kingston. I am not good about this whole overprotective brother shit."

"I'm not good at the annoying baby sister who tries to feed you too much shit."

"You're pretty good at being annoying though."

I shoved at him, but he didn't move, damn muscled man.

"As for me and Kingston, we're just taking it slow. We're friends first. We always have been. That's not going to change."

Hudson held me tightly, sighing into my hair. "Good. I just hope that remains true."

And with that ominous thought, I kissed his cheek, and then headed back out to girls' night. I didn't want to think about what would happen when Kingston and I broke up. Whatever did happen though, we had to just remain friends. Phoebe was with Kane, so that meant Kingston would always be in my life, even if things turned out horribly. But I didn't want to dwell on things that hadn't even happened yet, so I was going to push it out of my mind, and only think about time with the girls.

Of course, nothing was ever like I wanted it.

"So, how are you and Kingston?" Aria asked, and I frowned at her.

"You just saw us together. Things haven't changed." And why did I keep feeling butterflies every time someone mentioned him?

"I want details," she teased, sipping at her drink.

We were at an ax throwing restaurant thing, and I had no idea what I was doing. Daisy of course was winning, with Libby and Aria coming up second and third. Phoebe and I were not doing well. But that was fine, we were trying our best. Even though it didn't seem we were.

"I like it. The two of you are great together. And now we can easily double date without things being weird," Phoebe put in, as she picked up her ax and went to the target. She of course missed the board completely, and Libby took a photo, grinning.

"I'm going to send this to your man."

"Please do, because that means he can help me practice, and that means lots of cuddling."

"It's just like golf," Daisy said.

"You know, where they hover around you, and try to help you with your swing."

"Oh, so I guess I should invite Kingston?" I asked, as everybody cheered.

"You guys are just so cute," Libby said, as she sipped her drink. "It makes me actually believe love and happiness could happen." She paused and looked down at the single drink she had had all night. "Maybe I should switch to water."

"You *are* out of practice," Daisy said, handing over the water pitcher.

I sipped water as well, since I had had my one drink

for the night, and continued to play poorly at whatever ax throwing game we were trying to play.

"Hey, I have to go," Aria said, not ten minutes later, and I frowned at her.

"Is everything okay?"

She nodded, but I saw the tension in her gaze, and everyone else seemed to catch it as well. "I just have to pick up Travis."

"What's wrong with Travis?" Daisy asked, and I heard the biting tone. She apparently wasn't a fan either.

Aria seemed to have sensed it as well, and she lifted her chin. "He needs a DD."

"And he can't call a ride share?" Phoebe asked softly. "I mean...it's good he's calling you though. That way he's not behind the wheel."

"We're friends. I'm going to pick him up. It's what I do. At least he's not getting behind the wheel."

"Again," Daisy muttered, but Aria didn't seem to hear. Instead, Aria waved at us, and headed out, and I pressed my lips together, not wanting to say anything.

"Is she okay?" I asked.

Daisy shrugged. "I don't know. I can never tell with Aria. She's so closed off even when she thinks she isn't."

We sat there in silence for a few more moments, lost

in our thoughts and lives and the world continued around us.

"I need to go get Amelia. I keep getting kicked out of my own house so my parents can watch her, and I know they want me to have a life, but I miss my baby."

"I should go too," Phoebe said. "Kane should be home from work now. And well..." She blushed, and Daisy just laughed.

"I'm going to go see my kid and Hugh. You guys okay to drive?" she asked, her voice serious.

We all nodded and pointed to the fact that none of us had finished a drink. We finished paying, our girls' night now fully finished, and walked to our cars. We had all parked near each other, so we were still together when Libby came forward.

"So what is going on between you and my cousin?" Libby asked, and I cursed under my breath.

"Did you really think you were going to get through tonight without answering?" Daisy asked, and I knew she was trying to lighten the tone. We were all worried about Aria after all.

"I don't know. I had a huge crush on him, and I loved him in a sense where I knew I could fall in love with him. And now it's all different and he's real and I don't know what I'm doing. Is that enough?" I asked, speaking far too quickly.

The girls stared at me, before it looked as if a balloon had finally let out air, and they relaxed.

"Well. I love that stage of not knowing exactly where you're at. It's a good stage. It is horribly stressful, but you'll figure it out. I like the two of you together," Phoebe repeated.

"And maybe you should do something that I was really bad at, and actually talk to him about your feelings." Daisy winced as she said it, and I shook my head.

"Let's get through these first few weeks first before I blurt something crazy like I like him or something."

Libby just snorted. "I'm the worst at relationships so I have no words of advice, other than live in the moment for as long as you can, because reality is really harsh, and I hate it." She winced. "Okay, so I will not be giving any relationship advice."

We all said our goodbyes, laughing with one another, and I headed home, feeling a little lighter, and yet heavier at the same time.

My life was now intrinsically connected to these people who were also connected to Kingston. Falling for your crush, for a member of your friend group, was always wrought with terror and ample time for mistakes. And I needed to remember that.

I pulled into the driveway, double-checked my locks and security, and finally relaxed with a glass of wine and my planner. I still had a couple more hours of work to do, and soon Kingston would be calling, and we would have our nightly chat. But when the doorbell rang, I froze, panic settling in until I looked at the video readout and realized it was Kingston.

Now my heart was racing for a whole other reason.

I scrambled off the couch, setting my wine glass on the coffee table, and unlocked the multiple locks, and opening the door.

"Hey, I didn't know you were coming by."

Kingston smiled, lowering his head to brush his lips along mine. "I needed to stop by Home Depot and pick up a few things, and they had those LED lights that you were looking for that had been out of stock forever." He held out the box, and my heart tripped.

Damn it. He'd thought of me.

I had just casually mentioned it, and he had thought of me.

I was in deep trouble.

I pulled him inside and closed the door behind him. I locked one lock, one deadbolt, and tried to let out a deep breath, telling myself I didn't need to lock all three right now.

"It's okay. You can do it. I don't mind you locking everything and setting the security alarm. It's a good idea."

I bit my lip, still feeling a bit self-conscious. "Thank you. I hate that feeling of slight panic."

"You know what I do for a living, right, babe? I want you to keep safe. And if that's the locks and security that I installed? The better."

Relieved, I did indeed lock everything and set the security again, before I found myself pinned to the door, with Kingston's mouth on mine, and I groaned into him.

"Hello," he whispered.

"Hi there."

"I just wanted to stop by. I know we have a phone call later, but I needed to see you."

He always did things like that, surprising me. So I reached up and cupped his cheek.

"I'm glad you're here too. I missed you."

He smiled, lowering his face to mine, when his phone rang. "Damn it."

"It could be important. Come on, let's head to the living room."

"You're right, let me answer it real quick." He paused, his shoulders tightening. "It's the hospital," he said, as he met my gaze, and I swallowed hard, watching him answer. He didn't say much, just cursed under his breath, and when he ended the call, he stared at me, and rubbed a fist over his chest.

"I'm a match, but Buckley's too sick for the transplant to work right now. They need to get him better in order for him to even be able to get through the procedure."

My heart fell, and I moved forward, wrapping my arms around him. He immediately hugged me back tightly, resting his cheek on the top of my head.

"I'm so sorry."

"How the hell is he going to be able to get better in order to get medicine that's going to hurt even more? I don't fucking understand."

"I don't either. But you'll be there for him as soon as you can. He'll get through this. You both will."

"I just don't know," he whispered, and I held him close, knowing there was nothing I could say. But I was there for him, and it had to be enough for now.

13

CLAIRE

"I'm still a little surprised that we're on a date," I said, the words slipping out from my mouth before I even realized it.

Kingston took my hand and raised that very sexy brow of his.

"Really? Considering all we've done. You're surprised about the date?"

I blushed, and ducked my head as we made our way to the check-in of the ice-skating rink. I was not great at ice skating, although Kingston was as he had played club hockey in school, but I was going to try. If I accidentally cut myself or fell or broke a hip, I would just have to deal with it.

The fact that I could even look at the blades on those skates and not have a panic attack meant I was breathing through some trauma at least. *Therapy might be helping*. Another shocking event for the day.

"We go on dates," Kingston said with a frown, and I realized I may have said the wrong thing.

"We do dinner, usually at home because we're both working too hard, or we meet up with our friends when we're already out. I don't think we've done a full date that wasn't part of a larger plan. Not that it's a bad thing. I mean, I'm not complaining. We're both just so busy. And I like staying home. I like watching movies with you, even if we're watching them from two separate beds." My face fell as he continued to frown before he walked away to get us our skates. He went for hockey skates, while I got the figure skates. He knew my size without even asking. Had I told him? Or had he just known?

"Kingston?" I asked softly as we moved our way to the bench to put the skates on.

"I'm just thinking. You're right. I've never taken you out on a date."

"You have. In just our way. I mean we did start off on a cabin date."

"That happened accidentally because of a storm." He scowled once again, before leaning forward to take my chin between his thumb and forefinger and brushing his lips over mine. The sensation was so smooth, so soft, that my toes curled.

"Happy first date then," he whispered. "And I'll do better. Because I like dating you, Claire. Because maybe if we actually went on dates, you wouldn't look shocked every time someone calls you my girlfriend."

I shoved at him playfully, and unlaced my shoes so I could put on my skates.

"I don't look shocked."

"Your eyes go wide, and your mouth drops open, before you stumble your way into agreeing."

"And you seem perfectly okay with it. You don't freak out at all?" I probably shouldn't be asking these questions, especially not in public. But dating was so you could get to know one another. And while I knew Kingston because we had been friends for so long, I liked getting to know this version of him.

"I don't know, I worry about so many other things, something like being called a boyfriend doesn't bother me. Should it?"

"I'm not the right person to ask that considering I look like a guppy apparently every time someone mentions it." I laced up my skates, as Kingston's shoulders shook next to me.

"More like a goldfish."

"Jerk."

"But *your* jerk. At least according to other people."

He stood up first, and I did my best to pull my gaze from the way that his jeans molded his ass.

There was just something about Kingston Montgomery that did things to me. But that had always been the case with him, even when he hadn't seen me the way that I might have wanted before.

He held out his hand, and I slipped my smaller one into his calloused one and let out a sigh.

"I'm really not good at this."

"Dating or figure skating?"

"Let's go with both on that answer."

He let out a rough chuckle. "You'll get the hang of it."

"I really don't think I will. But I can try."

"That's all that I ask."

"That's asking a lot."

He kissed my temple, and I grinned, doing that wobbly thing on skates before we got onto the ice. My feet immediately went out from beneath me, and I fell hard on my ass. A couple of teenagers laughed, and Kingston ignored them, leaning over to pick me up without even sliding. The man was diabolical. And I was totally going to fall in love with him for real. That was going to be a problem.

"You okay? I'm sorry I didn't catch you."

"We're at the entrance, if you would've caught me, you would've had a blade up somewhere you didn't need to."

"Well that sounds lovely," he said, cringing.

"Let's just get out of the entryway so I don't embarrass us any further."

"You're doing just fine." He took my hand and set me next to the wall so that way I could hold on.

"Maybe I should have gotten hockey skates."

"You don't have the toe pick, but they are a bit easier for me."

"I feel like the toe pick will just make me fall. Case in point, that incident right when we got on the ice."

"I don't think that's the toe pick's fault."

"I would push you, but then I would probably be the one that fell, and I'd hurt a small child."

"You're doing just fine. Plus I get to hold you, I think it's a win-win."

"Look at you being all smooth."

"I try."

"So, you take a lot of dates out on ice skating rinks like this?" I asked despite myself. I seriously could have kicked myself, but then I would've fallen on the ice again and I already knew I was going to be bruised from it.

"Yes, just last week I was taking my other girlfriend out."

"You are very lucky that I know that you're joking with me, or I would've pushed you, my falling be damned." Not an inkling of jealousy slid through at his joke though, so was that progress? Or was that just denial?

"Okay, I think I've got the hang of it," I said, as I let go of the wall. Kingston held my hand, and when I wobbled, I leaned into him.

"There you go, you've got it!" Kingston practically shouted, and I ducked my head, blushing.

"Why are you so good at everything?"

"It's a gift."

"You were supposed to be modest."

"Have you met my family? There's no modesty in us at all. That's the whole point."

"I wonder how long this outdoor skating rink is going to be going for?" I asked. "Maybe I can take the niece and nephew out here."

"It should be open for a few more months. We haven't even hit the cold part of winter yet."

I shuddered since it was actually cold right now. And would probably stay cold through at least March. We had been known to get snowstorms in June before.

"They'll probably be better at ice skating than me."

"You're doing great. Just lean into me. I'll catch you this time."

"I love that you qualified it this time. And yes, maybe I'll bring the kids out, and Hudson too. He needs to get out of the house."

"He doing okay?"

I shrugged as we continued around the oval rink. "I think so. I mean, I don't really know if you ever get over that kind of grief, but more go through it. So it's always going to be there for him. But he has the kids and loves his job."

"He's a talented artist, I can't wait to actually get my tattoos."

"Oh yes, you had to postpone it right?"

"For Eddie, and then well, I'm going to continue to wait until we know more about Buckley."

I squeezed his hand and knew that we were all waiting for news about Buckley.

"Well, we'll just keep waiting. I want to get a tattoo as well, but I don't know who to go to. Everyone has such a long waiting list."

"Are you at least on the random waiting list?" he asked.

"I am. For the Legacy shop. Not the one down in Colorado Springs or in Downtown Denver. But for Hudson's."

"Would you have him do your tattoo?"

"Not for this one. I want one around the scar when it's ready, and I think it would be too much for both of us if it was him."

"All of them are trained to work with scarred flesh."

"Thankfully. They're all great at what they do. So maybe I'll just go with random and get whoever I get."

"So a Montgomery will be doing your tattoo then. Sounds like a plan."

"You do realize that Nick isn't a Montgomery, right?"

"He's married to a Montgomery, best friends to a Montgomery, and works with them. He's one of us now."

"That's a little worrying," I said with a laugh.

"Yes, but we can't help it." We continued around the oval a couple of more times, before my legs started to burn, and we went for hot chocolate. Of course Kingston was fine and didn't look tired at all.

I was the one that needed a breather, so I was grateful when he spoke first.

"What do you say to dinner?" he asked, as we made our way to his SUV.

"I'm honestly starving, but I think this hot chocolate may fill me up."

"I think I have a joke about that, but I'm just going to hold back."

I rolled my eyes. "You do realize that I grew up with a brother, right? I can dirty talk just as much as you."

"Prove it. Later."

I blushed and let him help me into the SUV. "You know I can hop in myself."

"And I like touching you. Deal with it."

Everything fluttered inside, and I told myself that

we were taking it slow, even though nothing felt slow. How about we needed to take it slow? That made a lot more sense.

We walked into a nice American restaurant that had a bunch of different plates that you could choose from, and a cool bar. We ended up in a booth near the back, but we could still see most of the rest of the restaurant since it was a horseshoe shape.

"I love it here. They have the best Korean ribs."

"They also have a quesadilla on the menu. I don't really know what mood they were going for."

"Everything and anything."

"Well, I'm starving, so let's share a couple of things? Are you okay with that?"

"Oh thank God." I laughed as I said it, and he just stared at me.

"A couple of guys that I've dated in the past never shared things. They only wanted what they had, and never even wanted to trade bites. And I want to taste everything. And I'm not one of those girls who will just order a salad and then steal all your fries. If I'm going to eat, I'm going to eat, but I also want to try it all."

"I like leftovers, so anything you want, we get."

"I don't mind sharing."

"Then I guess we're a perfect pair."

Again that flutter came back.

After we ordered our drinks, with the Korean rib

appetizer in between us, we just talked. About everything and nothing. With both of us going at full speed recently with work and life, it felt nice just to sit back for once.

"I still can't believe I missed the bear completely," Kingston said, and I laughed into my drink.

"I didn't even get to really see it. Only a glimpse of it, then I was shoved back into that bathroom. And that woman was mean."

"Meaner than the bear?"

"The bear just waddled past and didn't do anything. Although from the way Phoebe tells the story, she frantically ran and got into the first car she saw."

"Which happened to be Kane's."

"Well, that's a meet cute, right?"

"Damn straight. And I got to meet you that day too."

"And you barely even noticed me."

"I noticed you, Claire. But you were Phoebe's friend, and I figured it would complicate the situation if I hit on you while he was hitting on your friend. What if it didn't work out?"

Flabbergasted, I sat back in the booth.

"Are you serious right now?"

"Yeah, and then well, I didn't know what to say. And Phoebe and Kane got serious, and then they broke up, and things just got complicated."

"And I was too nervous to say anything at all."

"Well now we're here."

"And now we're here."

We finished our dinner, with both of us eating way too much food, but I couldn't help it, he'd gotten an extra meal, that way we could indeed try everything that we wanted, and it looked like he would be living on leftovers for the next couple of days. While we waited for the check and our boxes, I blinked when I realized I recognized a couple of people at the table across the way.

"Is that Aria and Travis?" I asked, my voice low. Kingston turned slightly so he could see and nodded.

"Yep. Looks like a double date."

"But I thought they were dating."

He shook his head. "No, they're just friends. Aria might feel something for Travis, but Travis has his head too far up his ass to see."

I raised both brows at him, but he didn't elaborate.

Before we could say anything, we got the check, and then packaged up all of Kingston's leftovers. As we made our way out, Aria waved at us, but didn't beckon us over. We gave her space, since we didn't want to make anything more awkward, but something just felt off.

"So where to next?" I asked, my heart in my throat.

"What do you say to dessert?" he asked, again raising that single brow.

"Is that a line?"

"Of course."

"Okay then, let's go."

His eyes widened for an instant, then he leaned over the center console, and brushed his lips against mine.

"Let's go."

And dessert might have taken all night.

Who needed sleep when you lived in the moment?

14

KINGSTON

I woke to a soft, warm body pressed against me and even though I hadn't slept for shit, and it felt as if a two-ton anvil was on my chest, I smiled. Claire lay on her side, one hand raised slightly to hold my own—something we'd both done in our sleep and hadn't even noticed. Her naked back lay against my front and every inch of her curves molded to my body.

This wasn't a bad way to wake up to be honest.

In fact, it was something I wanted to continue doing. Just like I wanted to continue running my hand up her thigh and then over her stomach to between her legs.

Claire awoke with a gasp, my fingers playing with her clit and then between her folds. "Good morning," she moaned, rocking into me.

"Good morning." I licked at her neck and bit down gently, loving the way she squirmed in my hold. She arched her back, pressing her ass firmly against my rock-hard erection and it was everything I could do not to slide into her right then and there. Instead, I held myself back, slowly bringing her to climax as she lay in my arms, the rising sun barely breaking through the blinds. And when her inner folds clamped around my fingers, I continued to move, loving the way she gasped my name.

As she writhed, I took the condom I'd left on the nightstand before and quickly sheathed myself before lifting her leg and sliding deep inside her. We both moaned and the movement, the feeling of her wet heat, was nearly too much to comprehend as I began to rock in and out of her.

"So. Full."

"I love this," I moaned and nearly froze, realizing what I'd said. But she hadn't seemed to hear as she moved against me, so I let those words slip by as I continued to move, each one of us nearing the peak.

I hadn't said *I love you*—but *this*. And while that was a difference, it was the closest I'd ever been to saying the true words. And as I nearly came to terms with what that meant, my orgasm finally shook me, my balls tightening, my release hard and fast. Claire's pussy pulsated around my dick, her hand reaching between her legs to press the V of her fingers around where we were connected, elongating the orgasm for both of us.

And when we could finally catch our breath, the words I'd whispered were long gone and merely a memory.

"I really like waking up that way. Just saying."

Laughing, I kissed her shoulder, not wanting to pull out of her, but knowing I'd need to deal with the condom. "Same." Another kiss. "What time do you have to work?"

"Most of the morning. I'm behind since I'm waiting on a distributor, but I'll make it work."

I nodded, though she could only feel the action. "I have a last minute install this morning, then I can come pick you up for the dinner. Does that work?"

She looked over her shoulder at me, our bodies still connected at the hips, and smiled. "That does. I'm glad we're doing this."

I looked between us and smirked.

"I meant dinner with the group, but yes, *this* was nice too."

I growled, pulling out of her so I could pin her back to the bed and slid between her legs. "Nice? You call that *nice*?"

"What? I meant that in a good way."

"Hmph." So in answer, I continued to make a feast of her, knowing that we were running late, but I didn't care. And when her thighs clamped around my neck and I finally had my fill of her taste if only for the moment, I figured this was anything but *nice*.

It was damn near perfection.

"CABIN PARTY TAKE TWO!" Phoebe announced as she popped the cork on the sparkling wine.

"Hey, I liked take one. Just saying." I sipped my beer as Claire laughed at me from across the room.

"Really?" she asked, her face blushing.

"Really." I couldn't keep my gaze off her, even as Lexington sighed dramatically next to me.

"And another one bites the dust," my cousin murmured under his breath.

I scowled at him as everyone else poured their drinks and milled about at the dinner. "Excuse me?"

"You don't see it, do you? The fact that you're clearly in love with Claire and now there's one fewer of us single guys out in the world. The Montgomerys and their ilk are dropping like flies, and I refuse to be one of them." Lex raised his chin as he spoke, just as Crew walked to our side of the room.

"Is he still complaining that people are being saddled up in some cattle drive of relationships?" the other man asked, and I shook my head at the both of them.

"You're ridiculous. First, there's nothing wrong with being in a relationship. Second, Claire and I...well... We're not there. We're not like the others." As she was on the opposite side of the room in deep discussion with Daisy and Hugh, I still kept my voice relatively low. I didn't want to hurt her by saying the wrong damn thing when I didn't even know what the hell I wanted— never mind what the hell I felt.

Lex grunted. "Whatever you say. Though with the way you two are spending so much time together? It doesn't seem very unsure to me."

"Hey, you know better than to ask a Montgomery about their feelings. Either they're at the point in life where they never shut up about it and force you to think about your own, our they cage themselves in and pretend feelings don't exist. You know the laws. There is no in between with you lot."

I shook my head. "First, you're starting to pick up Hugh's British sayings."

"I got it from *Doctor Who*, thank you very much," Crew said with a raised brow, his British accent dreadful.

"Second," I continued, ignoring him. "Your theory on Montgomery feelings isn't true."

"Eh, maybe it is." Lex shrugged at my glare. "But

seriously, man. You two look good together. Why fight it?"

"So says the man not in a serious relationship."

Crew and Lex gave each other a look that spoke volumes before Crew finally spoke. "And yet it seems you are."

"It's literally only been a few weeks. And we are at a party with family and friends. How about you just give me a break?" I asked, continuing to keep my voice low. There weren't that many fucking people in this room, and I didn't need everybody staring at me as I fumbled my way through whatever the hell I was doing with Claire.

"Okay, that's reasonable. I'm not an asshole. But I can be one if I need to." Crew winked before he went off to go annoy Phoebe and Kane. At least that's what I thought he was doing.

Since we hadn't been able to have a full event at the cabin, we were all here now, and trying to enjoy ourselves. Though like I had told Claire that morning, I had had a damn good time without the rest of them.

But I knew that we were all in the midst of our busy seasons, and this had been thrown together at the last minute. However, Claire and Aria were laughing in a corner, with Hugh standing near, with Daisy in his arms. We were all here, including Aria's friend Travis.

He had the bottle of champagne in his hands,

wiggling his brows at Aria.

"Dare me?"

Aria rolled her eyes. "No. Because it's bubbles, and it'll come through your nose again. We're not twenty."

"You're no fun." He still drank out of the bottle, and I met Crew's gaze. He just gave a slight shake of his head, and we didn't say anything. I wasn't part of that friendship, and I didn't know Travis well. But Aria knew what she was doing, and I couldn't be the asshole big brother all the time.

But I had a feeling if her actual brothers could see the way that Travis acted around her? Then I didn't think that they would be able to stand by. Not that I was doing a good job of it.

"Okay, we have appetizers, and dips. Mostly just things to dip. We have things to dip with, and dip for the dip. I think I've said dip enough times." Phoebe shook her head and reached for her water.

"And that's enough alcohol for me."

"One drink in, lame."

"You good, man?" Kane asked at Travis's words. Travis held up both hands, nearly dropping the half full champagne bottle.

"Yeah. I'm good. But I really wish we could have been at the cabin. With snow all around us. Would've been a really fucking good view. But this is nice. Whose house is this again?"

Aria gave a pained smile.

"We're at Crew's."

"Oh yeah. But you're not a Montgomery, right? Who are you here with?" he asked, swaying a bit.

He shook it off and grinned a little too widely.

"It's my house, so I guess you're all here with me."

"Hey there, can't believe you're just leaving me on read," Lexington said, as he wrapped his arm around Crew's shoulders. "And we're not even going to talk about last night." He fluttered his eyelashes, and Crew flipped him off.

"You're fucking weird, man. But I love you."

"Oh. That's cool. Love is love. But I don't like dick." Travis took another swig out of the bottle, and Aria gave us all a pained expression.

"Travis, stop being an asshole."

"You know I can't stop, babe."

I had no idea what Aria saw in that man, and I really didn't know what I was supposed to say in this moment, other than wanting to rip that bottle out of the man's hands and shake him until he figured out what the hell was going on.

Claire came up to my side, and I wrapped my arm around her.

"Okay, what dip are we going with?" I said, trying to ease the tension in the room.

"I made a quick and dirty spinach and artichoke dip. How about that?"

"I'm in." I kissed the top of her head, and ignored Crew and Lexington's looks, before we went back to eating.

"Did you hear that Livvy's friend tried to set her up on a date?" Daisy asked, and I shook my head. We were all lounging around the living room, Travis having calmed down once he'd had some water. He had made sure that Aria had a plate of food, and was smiling gently at her, as they were in the middle of a conversation with Crew. It was like night and day with that guy, and I did not understand him.

"Wait, with Livvy?" I asked pulling myself back to the conversation.

"With Livvy. She backed out of it, and I don't even know what her friend was thinking. But it was like a surprise blind date. Some guy just showed up."

"Oh my God. Is the guy okay?" Claire asked, and I frowned, looking at her, while Daisy burst out into laughter, Hugh just grinning into his drink. "What? I assume she kicked him in the balls?"

"No, but she almost kicked her friend in the balls. The guy had no clue what he was doing. I mean, they're friends and all, and the poor blind date guy was a little rude, but Livvy handled herself."

"We need to kick some ass?" I asked.

"You know that she won't let us handle anything. But I am tired of being on the outside when it comes to finding that bastard ex of hers."

"You know I could do it," Hugh said, playing with the rim of his glass. "No one would be the wiser."

"Just because you're not a Montgomery doesn't mean she won't murder you like family."

"I love how that made total sense. And I'm not taking the Montgomery name. I'll get the tattoo, but I'm not taking the name."

"Fine, but Montgomery is going to be my middle name."

"Montgomery's already your middle name." As her mom was the Montgomery, and that meant Daisy's last name was technically Knight.

"So you're going to keep Daisy and Knight and your middle names and then take Hugh's?" I asked, shaking my head. "That's a mouthful."

"I want the same last name as Lucy. Because whatever children that we decide to have later, they're going to have that name too. So it'll just make paperwork easier."

"And, she gets to have the longest signature known to man," Hugh said with a laugh, before kissing the top of her head.

"I hate the fact that it's always that women change their names, and men never really have to."

"My dad did," I said, speaking of Lincoln. "It made sense because the family they wanted to be connected to were the Montgomerys. But not everybody has to. Just like nobody has to get the tattoo."

"And yet I am being folded into the cult," Hugh said with a good-natured laugh.

"It's okay. We'll get you the pamphlet so you understand," Daisy said with a twinkle in her eyes, and I glared at her over Claire's head.

Daisy just wiggled her eyebrows, laughter dancing in her eyes, and I knew that she was going to harp on this.

"I mean, eventually Kane's going to make Phoebe an honest woman, and then she'll get the tattoo as well."

"Did someone say my name?" Phoebe said from the other side of the room. Between the music and the ten people talking at once, it was actually pretty hard to hear. Thankfully.

"We're just wondering when you're getting your tattoo!" Daisy called out.

Kane scowled, but I saw the nervous energy. Well then. It seemed like maybe she'd be getting the tattoo sooner than we thought.

And it was only because I knew Kane so well that I could even tell that. He gave a shake of his head, and I put my finger to my lips, promising I would keep the secret.

Kane was going to propose to Phoebe. That meant

Phoebe would be forever our family.

I shifted uncomfortably in my seat, because if Phoebe was part of it, Claire would be. But she was already with me. Why was I having such a fucking hard time with this? Why couldn't I just live in the moment.

"Not to bring down the conversation, but have you heard anything from the hospital?" Hugh asked, as everyone else moved on to their conversations.

Claire squeezed my hand, as Daisy wiped away a tear. I had told most of the people in this room about not being able to donate yet, and the whys of it. It was fucking heartbreaking.

"No. No real news. I get updates from the family. The mom made a group chat with everybody. I mean, I don't really know what I'm supposed to do other than just try to stay healthy."

"That's such a tough thing. I'm sorry, man."

"How is Buckley doing?" Claire asked.

"He's still sick."

"I meant emotionally. I know that they were talking about going with a foundation for a once-in-a-lifetime thing, but just day to day. Maybe we can give him a little party to lift his spirits? If his family agrees."

"Like make a video or something?" Daisy asked. "Or give him presents?"

"We can totally do that. Presents for the whole ward if we can," Claire answered, a little excitement in her voice. I shifted, both of us moving forward on the couch.

"I can talk with the staff member I've been working with at the hospital, see if there's something we could do last minute."

"As for Buckley, I know we might not be able to get into the room, depending on his white blood cell count, but maybe we can just do something for his family."

I looked down at Claire and kiss the top of her head. "You're fucking amazing."

"It's nothing. I just hate the fact that there's nothing you can do right now, so maybe there's something I can do. I plan parties for a living. I can plan this. Do you think you can give my number to his mom, too? Just so I can test the waters."

I brushed my thumb along her cheekbone, ignoring everyone else in the room.

"Let's see if it works out. Maybe not something big. Maybe we can do something."

"Anything. I'm there to help. Help all of you."

I brushed a kiss to her lips, ignoring the hoots and hollering at the gesture, and then settled back into the couch, Claire in my arms, and figured that this felt right.

Even if it felt as if we were moving at the speed of a bullet train, it felt fucking right.

And why did that scare me?

15

CLAIRE

"I still can't believe you guys are doing all of this. I'm just overwhelmed."

Buckley's mom reached out and patted Kingston's forearm, her eyes filling with tears. It was all I could do not to cry with her. My emotions had been all over the place these days, but crying in front of a woman who was in the middle of a circle of hell wouldn't help anyone.

"Of course we're here. And as soon as you feel like we're too much, we'll leave. I promise. We just wanted to do something." I heard the sound of defeat in his voice, and I knew that he was hurting. He wanted to do so much—*too* much. Maybe it was to try to do what he couldn't do for Eddie, or maybe it was just his way. I hated the idea that we would be too late, that we wouldn't be enough. But if we could put a smile on Buckley's little face, as well as make a few other children down on this ward laugh, then we would.

As soon as the idea for a little party had come to my mind, we had put plans in motion. That meant talking to Buckley's mom, as well as the staff on the children's cancer board. Just the idea of a children's cancer board made my stomach hurt because there was so much that we couldn't do. I couldn't cure cancer. I couldn't save a life. But I could bring a little joy, a little light in the darkness.

It honestly wasn't that hard of a job, other than thinking of something to do for Buckley since we couldn't enter the room he was in. He needed to be in a sterilized environment at least for now, with hope of a donation, so we took the party to the room right outside so he could still see us, and we could talk to him, and for the other children we had plans that the staff and care workers allowed us to bring in.

"We're here for however long you need us," I said, as Buckley's mother turned to me and smiled.

"Thank you so much. You guys are so creative, no balloons and clowns in sight." She shuddered. "I'm terrified of clowns, and someone decided to bring one along last time, and I'm afraid that my fear of clowns has moved on to my son."

"No, clowns are…a no," Kingston said as he visibly

shuddered. Watching a most likely six-foot four man with broad shoulders and all muscle shudder at the mere mention of a clown was one of the cutest things I had ever seen.

It was seriously hard not to fall completely and madly in love with this man.

"My brother and a lot of our friends are tattoo artists, so I figured temporary tattoos done by actual tattoo artists on those who want them, and children who can have the hypoallergenic fake ink would be perfect."

And the best part of all of it was that because I had found a printer who could make them on the fly for us, especially when I had told him what the temporary tattoos were for, each of the Montgomerys at Montgomery Legacy, Montgomery Ink, and Montgomery Ink Too, did personalized art for the children. Their parents had told us what some of their favorite things were, whether it was a comic book character, or an abstract piece of art. Just something to make them smile. Every single one of these kids were under the age of fifteen, and some of their favorites were of puppies and kittens with unicorns and rainbows, and it broke my heart because I knew that they were all hurting and putting on brave faces for us.

"I know a couple of the moms were a little skeptical

of you guys showing up with fake tattoos, but in the end, they know it's all just for fun. And safe."

"One hundred percent safe. We cleared it with all their doctors, and we'll be good."

"And we'll have Buckley's ready for him when he is all out of isolation," Kingston said, his voice low, full of promise.

"Yes. Exactly." Buckley's mother's voice broke ever so slightly, before she rolled her shoulders back and lifted her chin. Ever the strong mother who would not let anyone see her weak, or frail.

I reached out and squeezed her hand again.

"And every single kid here knows that once they're out of here and healthy and ready to play outside, they have full access for a one-of-a-kind trip through the Montgomery security jungle gym."

"Are you sure they're not going to be too small for that?"

"We've already been working with an engineer to make sure that we can modify anything that we need to. My cousins know what they're doing."

"Okay, good. I'm just so excited for all of this. I guess I needed a little bit of joy too."

"Of course you do. We're here for all of you. And we have three bakeries on the line who brought in food that all of you can eat as parents and family members, as well as food that's approved by their doctors that we think some of the kids can eat. We know not everybody is feeling up to it, but we have something if they want it and can have it. And later, just like with the obstacle course and jungle gym, they can come to the bakery and bake along with one of our family members."

"I've been to Icing and Cafe On the Rocks. I love them both. I can't believe that they're in your family."

I pointed to Kingston. "His family. I'm just a hanger on."

"Sorry, my mother already adopted you."

I rolled my eyes at that, even though my heart warmed, and Buckley's mother smiled so brightly, her eyes actually shone for an instant.

"You two remind me so much of me and my husband. He's at work right now because we need his medical insurance for this, or he'd be here with us."

"It's no problem. We'll save him a couple tattoos and a cupcake."

"Oh he might not get a cupcake. I looked at them before we got here, and I think they're mine now."

I knew she was putting on a front for us, but that was fine. We would do what we could for today.

In the end, we laughed with the children that we could, and waved at Buckley through the isolation in place. He was sitting up, and smiling, waving at us. His voice was a little raspy, and he still had dark circles under his eyes, but his mother had said he looked better. I wanted to believe that was true, and not just a mother's hope, or wanting to make us feel better or to alleviate our worries.

I wanted him to be safe.

There were children with caps on their heads, and bright pink wigs. Giggling fourteen-year-olds with braces and tubes all over their bodies. There was a small little toddler in a crib, bouncing on her feet, as she had one of those feeding tubes that broke my heart. But she clapped her hands at us, and we said our hellos and she got her sparkling little unicorn.

Every single one of the parents hugged us, even the ones that were a little skeptical about a bunch of bearded and tattooed and pierced people showing up. We probably weren't the normal crew to show up on a random Thursday to try to make kids smile. We did our best to stay out of the way, and our best not to break down.

Phoebe and Kane were there, as well as Leif and Nick and Hudson and Sebastian. We hadn't wanted to overwhelm them with us, and we promised we would be back.

From the way Leif was mad texting the group chats, I had a feeling there was probably going to be a new Montgomery plan in place for future visits, and not just this hospital. And not just this wing.

This was why I loved this family. And this was why I was falling in love with Kingston.

On our way out as Kingston went to go talk with Leif, I pulled my brother to the side, honestly surprised to see him here.

"How are you holding up?"

My brother looked off into the distance, the sharp peaks of the Rocky Mountains bright white with snow. He was silent for so long I was afraid I had made a mistake. Not just by asking him, but by bringing him along at all.

"I'm glad I came." He cleared his throat, and looked down at me, his eyes watery. "I miss her. With everything that I have. I miss her. I see her in our kids, and I see her every day. Every time I close my eyes. And when I wake up in the morning, I still feel like she's right beside me. Even though she's never lived in that house. She never got to see this house. But she's no longer in pain. And my kids don't get to know the woman that I loved. But those kids in there? I have to believe that they're going to survive. That they can beat this. Because I need them to get out of those walls. I need them to run around with my kids. But seeing them? It reminds me that there's still a fight out there. And maybe I should join. You know?"

Tears were freely streaming down my face at that

moment, and I hugged him tightly, ignoring his cursing as he reluctantly held me back.

"I'm fine, little sister."

"Well I'm not. So hold me."

"Your big buff boyfriend is on his way to do so as well. You're okay."

"I need those little kids to be okay. But I don't think they all will be. The math just isn't there."

"Then don't think about that. Think about the joy that you brought them today. It's all we can do in this moment. Always. You did a good thing here today. And from the way that those parents seemed to relax just for an instant? You gave them peace."

"And we're going to try to keep doing it," Kingston said as he came forward.

"I was just thinking that you would. Is Leif already on the plans?"

"He contacted his mother, and Aunt Sierra and Uncle Austin can do anything."

"I'm surprised you guys don't already have a foundation in your name. What with all the hospital visits I hear you guys have."

I knew Hudson was trying to lighten the mood, and I was grateful for it. My brother let me go and I leaned into Kingston instead.

"We have one, but it's to provide meals for children in schools, as well as housing for families in need after natural disasters, and we have another section that works well for women and families that need to get out of bad situations at home. It's not much, we're all smaller parts of a whole, but we do some things."

"Your family is out of this world."

"There's just a lot of us. We can't help it. We have been the recipient of good tidings and people who care about us over the years. So we're trying to do the same."

"I know that we're not going to be able to save every single kid. But I want to believe we can."

"I would say I need a drink, but I need to go pick up the kids. You're going to stop by later?" Hudson asked.

"I might. I have a work call later tonight."

Both men raised their single brows, and once again, I was jealous.

"You've worked how many hours on this?"

"And I would do it all again. But there's an event in three days, and Trix is handling most of it, because I'm trying to give her more responsibility, but I do have things to do. It's okay. I'm not overworking."

"See that she doesn't," Hudson said, and Kingston lifted his chin in acknowledgement.

"Don't worry. I will."

"Okay, I really don't like you two working together against me."

"Weren't you the one that worked with Oliver

against me in order for me to actually take a Sunday off?" Kingston asked.

"That was different. That was your little brother annoying you."

"And this is your big brother annoying you," Hudson said, as he tapped my nose.

"Call tonight. The kids miss you."

"I saw them yesterday. And I miss them already."

"It's a good thing we all live close then. Love you, little sis." He kissed my forehead, then headed off to his car. And after we said our goodbyes to everyone else, I found myself sitting next to Kingston in his SUV on the way to his house.

"That was tough," he said after a moment.

"It was tougher than I thought it was going to be."

"I need that little kid to be okay. Even if it's not me. Even if they find another donor, or it turns out he doesn't even need one, I need him to be okay. I don't need to be the one that saves the day, I just need someone to do it."

"I never thought you were the one who needed to put on a cape for the acknowledgement. You just throw yourself in when it's needed. It's not for praise. If anything you get embarrassed if anyone praises you."

"I'm not quite sure I like the psychoanalyzing," he said through gritted teeth, and I leaned over to squeeze his knee.

"Kingston."

"Claire," he said in the same tone, and we both sighed simultaneously.

"You haven't had a nightmare in a couple nights," he said, and I blinked at the change in subject.

"Where did that come from?"

"I said the word psychoanalyzing, and then my brain went down the therapy trail."

I winced but got out of the car at the same time as he did.

"I haven't, but I never know when they'll show up. I'm doing better now. Maybe just time?"

"If you ever want to talk about it, I'm here. I don't know if I'm the best one to actually have an answer. But I'm a sounding board."

"I know you are. And no, I don't have that many nightmares anymore. But I still go to therapy."

"Therapy helps."

"Do you go?"

He shook his head, and I frowned.

"I thought you did."

"No, Kane does. But I haven't really needed it."

"You're not serious, right?"

"What? I talk with you, I talk with my family, I talk with everyone at work. I don't know why I need to talk to anyone else."

"Because you keep blaming yourself for everything

that happens around you, maybe?" I hadn't meant to let that slip, and my voice had risen just slightly.

He looked taken aback and shook his head. "I don't take on the weight of the world."

"I beg to differ."

"Claire, I'm tired. After a long fucking day, and seeing all those kids? I don't want to talk about it."

"Maybe you should. Maybe not with me, but you lost your friend. You should talk to someone."

"I did. I talked to you. I talked to my parents. I'm fine."

I nearly asked him what fine meant to him, and then realized right now was not a good time. He was angry, annoyed, and hurting.

"Since my car's here, I'm just going to pack up my things and head home. I have a lot of work to do."

"Claire, you don't have to go. We were going to have dinner. Just hang out and veg."

"It's been a hard day. I'm just going to give you some space."

He cursed under his breath, and then came toward me. I looked up sharply, and he stopped in his tracks, holding up both hands.

"Did I startle you? I'm not angry. Well, I'm pissed off at the world. About the fact that whatever deity is out there can just give this kid cancer and there's nothing I can fucking do about it. I'm angry about that, but I'm not angry at you. You're allowed to call me on my bullshit, you know."

"I just don't want to upset you."

"Upset me. Yell at me. Be mad. I'm kind of an asshole sometimes."

"But you aren't though. That's the problem. You are a nice guy."

"I don't really like the term nice guy."

"You're not the trademarked term of being a predator. Not that kind of nice guy," I said, exasperated. "But I don't want you to carry everything on your shoulders and deep inside or whatever metaphor you want to use."

"Just don't go, okay?"

He didn't answer the question, not that I had even had one.

"Just stay? I don't think you should be alone either. Not after today."

I sighed, then moved forward, wrapping my arms around his waist.

"Today was good, but it also sucked."

"Majorly."

And when he rested his cheek on the top of my head, I knew I was in trouble.

Because I was falling in *love* love. As in already there. Rock bottom, and terribly in love with a man who I was afraid didn't love me back.

But before I could dwell too much on my emotions, his phone rang.

"Answer that, I'll go figure out what we're going to order to eat because I don't think either of us want to cook."

"Sounds like a plan." He kissed me softly, and then answered.

"This is Kingston."

He froze for an instant, and I looked up at him, eyes wide as this bright smile spread over his face.

"Just tell me the time. I'm there."

I moved forward, hugging him tightly, knowing exactly who he was talking to.

And when he ended the call, he picked me up by the waist and spun me around.

"His counts are up. We're doing the donation. Fuck yeah. We're not going to fail this time. We're going to fix this."

"Kingston."

He kissed me hard on the mouth.

"I know. I know. But we're going to try, okay? We're going to try."

And I held him, and hoped to hell it would be enough.

16

KINGSTON

Donation the third time around wasn't as easy.

I had been forced to stay the night for observation since my blood pressure had spiked, and then I'd been nauseous for most of the evening. Complications and side effects were always going to be an issue, but if it could help Buckley, I'd do it again and again—though I was pretty sure my body was done. I wasn't sure that I would ever be able to donate again, mostly because everything hurt like a bitch.

I lay on my couch, notebook in hand as I went through a couple of the scenarios for Noah and our next op, but all I really wanted to do was try to find a better position on the couch.

"You have an adjustable bed, why aren't you using

it?" Claire asked as she walked into the living room, two cups of tea in hand.

Grumpy and in pain, I closed my eyes. "Don't make me drink tea. Tea's for when I'm sick."

"You're not feeling well, and your mom told me to make you tea. So I'm listening to Mrs. Montgomery."

I opened my eyes and a smile slid over my face. "It's true. I would listen to her too. She's scary."

"You're very lucky I'm no longer on the phone with her. Because she would've heard that."

I winced, and then did so again when I accidentally shifted on the couch. Claire rushed over as quickly as she could with two hot cups of tea.

"What's wrong? You really need to be on the bed."

Ignoring the pain, I raised a brow. "Look at you trying to get me into bed."

"There is no way you and I are having sex," she said with a laugh. "I mean, you're amazing in bed and all, but I'm not about to break you."

"You're so sweet. Worrying about breaking me. Which I'm pretty sure we could make a case for the counterpoint."

"So full of yourself, and you won't even sit on your own bed that will adjust to your pain levels."

"I don't work well in bed. I never did my homework in my bedroom either. It's a thing. I want that to be a space for just relaxing." I raised a brow. "And fucking. You know, all the cardio I need."

"Are you still on pain meds? You're a little loopy."

I shook my head. "No, I'm just itchy or something. Need to get out. See the world. Maybe go ice skating again."

The laugh that escaped her mouth should have hurt, but she looked too damn cute. "There's no way we're going ice skating right now. You need to heal. Rest. You've done two donations this year. And your body was amazing enough to replace what you had the first time. Give it some space to do it again. For yourself."

"I know. I'm just a little claustrophobic."

"I can open a window." She ran her hand through my hair, and I nearly leaned into her palm like a cat.

This was so weird, having her here and making it feel normal. But it was normal. It wasn't like Claire was new in my life. But I'd never had a serious girlfriend to the point that she would be here while I was sick. Or practically have a drawer since she was taking care of me.

Claire had a drawer in my house. When the hell had that happened?

Then again, I had one over at her place, because it was just easier. Suddenly my chest started to tighten up, and it had nothing to do with recovering.

"You don't have to work, you know. You can just lie

in bed, watch a movie, do anything other than sit on this couch where you're clearly uncomfortable."

"I'm fine. I want to get these things done for Noah. We have more cases than usual on the docket, and I want to do my part. I'm co-owner and all."

"You are. And you do a lot. And you're allowed to take a break."

"I did the first time. And I took a couple of days off for this. Now I'm just going to work on paperwork. Since I can't get out in the field. Or get on a ladder."

"You're not going to get on the field anytime soon, are you?" she asked, a slight panic in her voice.

"No, but I will, you know." I paused and reached out for her hand. "You know sometimes that I have to go out and play bodyguard, right? That is my job to keep my client safe? You're okay with that, right?"

For some reason, we had never talked about that. Despite how many hours a day we spent together, or the fact that she had been someone I had protected in the past, we didn't talk about my job.

"Of course," she said softly. "I know what you do. You've taught me self-defense. You're *still* teaching me self-defense, for that matter. I'm okay with you being in danger, as long as it's not every day. Plus, it's not my place, I don't have a right to tell you what your job is. You do the work of your heart. At least I think so. I'm not saying this right."

"I do like what I do. I like making sure people are safe. Whether it's setting up a security system or being the one that's out in the field. My cousins do a little more of the technical work, the cyber security things, but that's not me. I just don't want you to worry that I'm out there."

"I do realize that you're in a position where you've literally been blown up before, just like your cousin, but I'm going to worry. You can't make me hold back from that. Just like your family worries."

"I was only blown up once." I paused. "Okay twice, but I wasn't technically in the room for the second one."

Her eyes widened. "What?"

"What?" I said again, and she ran her hand over her face.

"Maybe you can go back to just doing paperwork forever." She grinned as she said it, and I knew she was joking, even if part of her was telling the truth. My mother and fathers did the same thing. They didn't want me out there. And it wasn't as if I shot up the bad guys or arrested people. I had never fired a gun other than on the range. That wasn't what I did. I made sure the people who were around me were safe and got them where they needed to be. I wasn't James Bond.

And when I told Claire that, she just rolled her eyes. "You do like martinis though."

I nearly shrugged, then remembered the twinge. "Because I like olives with blue cheese. That's really the only reason to drink just pure vodka."

"So you don't do gin?"

I shook my head. "No, I've only done vodka. Now I feel like I should have done a gin martini. Maybe that would be different."

"I don't know, most gin tastes like Pine-Sol to me."

"I think we need to get you the right gin." This felt weird—as if we'd been sitting like this, having normal conversations all of our lives.

She smiled then, before handing me my tea. "Drink this. So that way I don't have to lie to your mother."

"Fine. For Mom. But you have to drink yours too."

Her eyes widened. "How did you know she told me to?"

"Because you're drinking tea when I know you like coffee more."

"There's nothing better than a latte with caramel drizzle. Sugar and I are best friends." She kissed her fingers in a chef kiss, and I grinned, clinking my mug to hers.

"To getting off this couch."

"You can go to bed anytime you want."

"Only if you're with me." Her eyes went dark for a moment, and I reached out, playing with her hair. "You've been spending a lot of time over here, helping me. Hell, most of the past weeks have been about me, my family, planning a party, and then working with Buckley and the whole ward. Are you having time for yourself? With your friends?"

"It's weird that all my friends are pretty much your friends too. So I do spend time with them. And I'm working. My life isn't all about you, I promise. But I don't mind part of it being about you. I like you." She pressed her lips together, as if wanting to say something more, and I swallowed hard, my chest tightening once again, this time forcing me to set my mug down.

"Claire," I began, and she held up her hand.

"It's fine. I know you're not feeling well, and we totally don't need to talk about feelings. It would just feel out of place right now."

"I haven't felt like this before."

I knew as soon as I said the words, I had said the wrong thing. Her face fell just for an instant, before she smoothed out her features again, and sipped her tea.

"You don't have to say that."

"Claire."

"You really don't have to say anything. You're healing, and we're waiting on news from Buckley's family. So why don't we just get back to work, okay?"

I was doing this all wrong. I just hadn't let myself think about what I felt for her. Because I wanted Claire. I wanted her in my life, and I liked her a lot. But what was love? What was that feeling? Shouldn't you just know? Considering how many people in my life were in healthy, loving relationships, you would think I would know exactly what that meant, but I didn't. Was it this heart-wrenching feeling that caused me pure panic? Was that love?

"I care about you," I blurted, wanting to say something. Anything. How was I supposed to know if I was in love with her? Why wasn't there a manual on this?

She flinched at the words, then she set her tea down very carefully.

"Shit. That is the worst fucking thing to say. I know that, I'm sorry."

She shook her head. "I haven't felt like this before either. So don't apologize." Her words were so clipped, icy, that I was afraid that she'd walk away.

"Claire, I just..."

"Don't. Those are your feelings. And mine are my own. I care about you."

"What are your feelings?" I asked, knowing that maybe if I latched onto those, I'd be able to figure things out.

I didn't want to do this wrong. I didn't want to hurt her. But hell, I didn't have a transcript for this. There wasn't anything I could say other than I wanted her in my life. And I didn't want her to walk away. Was that love?

"Those are mine until I figure them out," she said as she stood up. "And I've really put you in a spot when you can't even escape. And this was totally not the right time for this conversation." Her alarm went off as soon as she said it, and she smiled brightly, her eyes a little manic. "And now I have to go to work."

"Fuck. Claire." I tried to get up and groaned at pain rocketing up my back.

"Stop. Just sit down. We're okay. You and me, we're okay," she said quietly as she leaned toward me.

"Are we?" I whispered.

"We are. And I really do need to get to work. I have a meeting that I can't get out of. A huge event that's going to bring me a lot of future business, I hope. And we sort of stumbled into this conversation that doesn't feel very organic. So we'll talk about it later, okay? We're fine." She kissed me softly, so I cupped her face, and deepened the kiss, desperation in every movement.

"Come back?" I whispered.

"Of course." Then she brushed her lips against mine, and left, leaving me alone on the couch, realizing I had just stepped in it so hard that I knew I would have to grovel worse than ever to get back.

How the hell had things turned so quickly?

And where the hell had I gone wrong?

My door opened again before I could even figure out

how to get off this couch and run after her, and hope spread through me.

"Claire?" I called out.

"No it's just us," Kane said as he and Crew came inside.

"We're on shift to babysit you with Claire at work. Sorry we're a little late." Crew closed the door behind both and frowned at me. "What the hell did you do?"

I held up both hands ignoring the pain in my side. "I really fucked up."

"Oh hell. Did you break her heart?" Kane asked, before throwing himself in my armchair. "Phoebe is going to kill me if you hurt Claire. Do you understand that? That woman is the love of my life. I'm going to propose to her as soon as everything calms down and we're through the next crisis. But hell, there's always a fucking crisis in this family. What the hell did you do to Claire?"

"I didn't do anything." That sounded petulant but I needed to catch up to my damn thoughts.

"Now that's a lie," Crew said as he sat in the opposite chair from Kane. "Let me guess, things got too real, and you got too scared?"

"I don't like the mocking tone from a man who isn't in a relationship," I bit out.

"Fine. I'm just going to sit back and watch you Montgomerys fuck up everything again. It takes you forever to realize what you're feeling, and then you don't say the words."

"Daisy really hurt you that bad?" Kane asked, and I froze, not realizing where this conversation was heading.

Crew let out a mocking laugh. "No. I'm not talking about me. I'm doing just fine. Daisy and I are friends. That's all we ever should have been."

Then who the hell was he talking about? I didn't ask. "Now that we're done dissecting Crew's love life, can you help me figure out mine?"

"Well, did you tell her you love her?" Crew asked.

I looked at him, my mouth gaping like the goldfish that I had joked with Claire about earlier.

"I'm going to take that as a no," Kane said as he pinched the bridge of his nose. "How could you fuck that up?"

Scowling, I leaned forward. "So says the man who broke up with Phoebe before."

"And I groveled. I fucked up there. And we're better than ever. She's going to be my wife."

"Did you get a ring?" Crew asked.

"Yes. It's hiding in Dad's safe."

"Good place for it. When are you going to propose?"

"After the party. That way she can enjoy time with the family, and we don't take attention away from everyone getting together, you know? Plus there's new babies around, and I don't know, I just want it to be the two of us." Kane then glared at me. "Because I love her. Just like you love Claire. All of us can see it."

He made it sound so easy when it was anything but. "How do you know? How do you know if you love someone."

"I used to think if you had to ask that, it wasn't really love," Crew began, and held up his hands as I scowled at him. "But that would be wrong. Because love isn't a single thing. There are thousands of poems and books and movies about it, and you just never know. You don't know until you're feeling it. I don't even know if I've felt it," he countered, and it looked like Kane wanted to ask who. "But it doesn't have to be this cupid heart love bomb bullshit. It can just be the fact that you care about a person."

"That's what I told her."

"Oh my God," Kane said, putting his hands over his face. "You said you *cared* for her?"

I winced, as Crew stood up and began to pace. "That is after I said I had never felt like this before," I put in, knowing that I was digging my own grave with platitudes.

"Next time just say it's not you it's me, and add a few other cliches, why don't you?" Crew asked.

"We weren't even really talking about it. And then I just blurted it out. Because I needed to say something.

Because she's been so amazing and caring, and she does everything she can to help everyone around her. And I wanted to say something about how I felt but then I didn't know and then it was there, and I couldn't stop myself."

"I want you to think about what you just said and think about the words that you weren't saying," Kane whispered.

"Tell me this," Crew said after a moment. "Where do you see yourself in the next month? With Claire?"

I didn't even pause in my response. "Of course."

"There's not an 'of course' if you're worried about what could be," Kane put in.

Crew shook his head. "Where do you see yourself in a year? With someone else?"

"No. I can't think of myself with anyone else. I'm with Claire."

Kane sighed. "Do you see yourself moving in together? Or sharing a drawer?"

"We already have drawers in each other's houses…" I answered, feeling more like an idiot with every passing second.

"Where do you see yourself in five years? With her or without her?" Crew asked. "Or does the thought of even thinking that far ahead without her hurt?" I rubbed my hand over my chest, and Crew clucked his tongue at me. "Bingo."

"You fucked up," Kane said pointedly.

Everything clicked and I realized I was an idiot. "Oh my God, I'm in love with Claire."

"Oh no, this is brand new information," Crew said deadpan, and I flipped both of them off.

"I need to tell her. Can I call her?"

"You really shouldn't do that over the phone or even a text after you screwed up," Kane answered.

"But the party's tomorrow, and everyone's going to be there. She has to go in early because she's planning it, and I said I would meet her there. She's not even coming over tonight."

"Then tell her tomorrow. Find a way to make it so you can be on your knees and grovel when you do," Kane added.

"Of course you love her." Crew stared at me.

I looked at Crew at the simplicity of his words. "How is *this* of course?"

Kane looked between us. "Because you wouldn't be so worried about how to fix this if you weren't. You were so worried about being wrong so you wouldn't hurt her, that you didn't realize it was right."

Kane cleared his throat. "When did you get all philosophical?"

"I have no idea. I really need to get laid," Crew said, breaking the tension, and I ran my hands over my face.

"I need to tell her. Tomorrow. I need to fix this."

"You really do," Kane put in.

"Tell her at the party. She'll be there in a pretty dress, you can dance around, there will be twinkle lights I suppose, and just do it."

"But what if she doesn't love me back."

And that right there told me exactly what I'd been fearing this entire time. Kane just glared at me, but it was Crew who gave me that look of pity.

"I think she does. Kane thinks she does. All of our circle thinks she does."

"But your love of her isn't contingent on her loving you. Tell her for the both of you. And if she doesn't say it back, that doesn't make your feelings any less meaningful. But fix this, okay? Because both of you deserve to hear it."

And with that, Crew pulled out his phone, ignoring us, and I just stared at Kane, wondering where the hell Crew had gotten all that information.

I needed a plan to make things right.

I had fallen in love with Claire Harlow.

And I might have just broken her heart.

17

CLAIRE

"I honestly don't know how we could have pulled this off without you. You are a godsend." Holland wrapped her arm around my shoulder and squeezed, only I ducked my head.

"You guys know exactly what you're doing. You would've figured it out."

"We would've made it work because in the end it doesn't matter what fairy lights or food or entertainment we have. We just need each other at these events. However, it's also nice to make them special."

My chest warmed and I wasn't sure if it was the praise itself, or the fact that it was Kingston's mother who gave it. "You were the one who helped us set up the extra lighting, and the catering since we had to move to a different suburb and our old catering couldn't accommodate us."

She shook her head and squeezed my shoulders again. "We used to do a potluck, where everyone brought something, and the spreadsheets were insane. And sometimes for reunions or other parties we do. But other times we want to feel a little pampered. And that's what today's all about. Thank you for helping my family feel special."

"It honestly wasn't that hard." And I wasn't lying. They had most everything set up. I was only there to handle a little of the loose ends that slipped through the cracks because of the change in venue. And it was because I happen to have contacts, thanks to my job. And in the end, I had made more contacts for different vendors and services. And a few of Kingston's aunts and uncles had taken my information for help with their own get togethers. And not just with personal events, but with their businesses.

And when I explained that to Holland, she grinned.

"We like taking care of our own."

"Honestly, I feel like I'm gaining the most out of this." I smiled, my heart warming at the thought of being their own. Even as it kicked just a little bit. Because I hadn't seen Kingston yet.

He had called me to say goodnight, and I had answered. Because not answering would've made our odd little disagreement a spectacle. And maybe it wasn't even a disagreement. Maybe it was just the two of us realizing we were in two different places. It wasn't as if I could force him into loving me. Or force him into speeding up that realization. It hadn't been the correct time, and I don't even know why I freaked out the way that I had.

We had arrived separately since he had had to deal with a few work things beforehand so he could have the weekend off to help me at my event the next morning. And I had come in early to do my part of the job. I had a huge weekend in front of me, with not only this event, but the biggest one to date tomorrow evening that I would have to start in the morning. Trix couldn't handle it herself, and that was fine. It was my business after all. And as I had slid this party in the middle of my work schedule, I was a little overwhelmed, and not just personally.

"Usually we just throw some cheese on the table and call it a day. This is much better," Ethan Montgomery said as he winked at me.

"I heard about your family and cheese."

Ethan rolled his eyes. "It's oddly a little weird that people do know our love of cheese. It could be the shirts and branding we wear."

"I love a good baked brie, perhaps in a pastry shell with either a spicy chili jam or even a fig jam on it.

Well, and a little Havarti. And a good Asiago. And of course parm. Parmesan is on everything." I was rambling now, and Ethan put his hand over his heart.

"You're literally a woman after my own heart. I mean, I'm already married to two people and you're my son's girlfriend, but I still love you."

"So smooth," Holland said, shoving at her husband playfully.

"What? I wanted to say that I loved her without being weird about it. And of course it got weird."

It was like a kick in the shin to hear Kingston's father being so open with his feelings. But then again, finding love and friendship and admiration was a different kind of emotion. And it had a different weight to it. I knew that. I had never been in love.

I put on a brave face and pushed back those thoughts. No need to bring Kingston and the weirdness into this conversation. "If all it takes is for you to love cheese to be adopted into the Montgomery family, it's a little telling. And explains so much."

Holland smiled, everyone else laughing as she studied my face. "Are you okay, Claire? I know you've been working double time for all of your events. Did we ask too much? We're forever grateful. But if you need to go home and get some sleep, or just sit down and relax, please do. In fact, I'm going to make it mandatory that you go relax."

She hugged me tightly, as Aria skipped over to me, literally skipped. "You are remarkable. I'm so happy you were available to help out. Mostly because your help meant I didn't have to. I suck at this." She turned to Holland and Ethan. "Do you mind if I steal her?"

"Go. Make sure she has fun and relaxes. Where is Kingston?" Holland asked, and my heart raced.

"Oh, he just got here." Aria squeezed my hand, and now I had to wonder if she knew. Did everyone know?

No, people were just arriving, and the event was just beginning. It wasn't out of the ordinary for us to arrive separately because I was helping set up. But why did I feel like everybody knew that something was awkward between us?

"I'll talk to you soon," I said to the others, and let Aria drag me over to where Livvy and a couple of Aria's other cousins were.

They said their names, and I knew I was never going to remember everybody. As it was a family event, no one wore name tags, and really, they should by now. Or maybe they should literally just get their names tattooed on them so that way we would always know who was who.

"You look wonderful," Livvy said with a soft smile.

I looked down at my sparkly gray dress and blushed. "It had to be something I could move around in, and this is one of my normal wedding outfits actually."

"It looks great, *and* I saw the cheese table," Aria put in, wiggling her eyebrows. "You do know us."

I waved her off. "That was all Kingston's mom. You guys already had that set up."

Livvy laughed. "That's pretty much on standby."

"Did you know a few of us are actually lactose intolerant?" Aria asked, and I blinked.

"Is that even allowed?"

Aria snorted. "It is. And a couple of us don't particularly love cheese, but we don't say that out loud."

"Because you get bullied? That doesn't sound like you guys."

"No, because you get teased, and then we buy you your favorite thing. It's what we do." Livvy sipped her drink and looked over my head. "And it looks like we're about to lose you."

I turned quickly, my stomach doing somersaults as Kingston came forward. He had on black suit pants and a gray button-up shirt. He had rolled the sleeves up to show his forearms, as well as his ink, and I nearly groaned. There was just something about that man.

"I think she was lost to us long before this," Aria muttered under her breath, but I ignored her.

"Hey," I whispered.

"Hey." He reached out and slid a strand of my hair behind my ear, as both Aria and Livvy sighed behind me. "You did a great job. Sorry I couldn't help."

"You've been a little preoccupied. I can't believe you went back to work today."

"Just for a little thing. And I was sitting down for most of it. I'm feeling better. Hardly a twinge."

My teeth bit into my lip as I reached out and slid one finger in his belt loop, ignoring everyone around us. "Well, if you need to sit down, you should."

"You're the one in high heels after running around all day trying to help my family. You amaze me."

I swallowed hard, my pulse racing. "Any news?" I asked, my mind going a thousand different directions and landing on Buckley.

Kingston shook his head, but his small smile didn't falter. That was something at least. "We won't have news for a while. But I'll let you know as soon as I do." He lowered his head and brushed his lips against mine. "Are we good?" he asked, his voice low.

And he was still touching me, still wanting to be with me. I needed to get over myself. "We are." And when I smiled, it was truthful. This wasn't even a bump, just us trying to breathe.

"Hello. We're here too," Aria said with a laugh, and I let go of Kingston to turn to face them.

Kingston in turn put his hand on my hip, and I blushed. "Hello there. *All of you.* Where's Amelia?"

Livvy just smiled and shook her head. "She's with Mom and Dad. They kidnapped her."

"Got to love grandparents."

"I know, right? In fact, all of the kids are with their grandparents. That means we parents are allowed to have a little fun."

I gestured toward her sparkling water. "Do you want me to go get you a drink?"

"First off, you've done so much, you don't get to wait on me. And no, I'm in the mood for mocktails tonight. And now I'm going to go see my brother. I haven't seen him in a couple of weeks, and I promised him I would annoy him today." Livvy walked off, and then another one of Kingston's cousins joined us, and then another.

Aria left at some point, and I realized that Travis had shown up. He had a drink in his hand and was swaying a bit in her arms as they danced. He smiled down at her and I saw stars in Aria's eyes. Maybe something good was coming from that situation after all?

"I love everything that you've done," Daisy said as she came forward and gave me a tight hug. "I realize that we Montgomerys are a little insane, and a little overwhelming, but thank you for making this party happen."

"You should stop thanking me. Kingston's family did most of it."

"And my mom would credit you," Kingston countered.

"I'm just glad I was able to help with what I could."

"We've all been through so much, and with everything happening around us, it's nice just to get together," Raven said, her hand on the small swell of her belly. Sebastian had his arm around her, his attention finally pulled off Aria.

"I have noticed that things tend to happen around you guys."

Noah came forward then, with his spouses, Greer and Ford on either side of him. "You too, Claire. But it's fine, in the end we get cheese and cake. But not together. We do have some standards."

I shuddered at that thought. "Although there is a cheesecake."

"Did someone say cheesecake?" Hugh asked as he came forward and wrapped his arms around Daisy.

Kingston squeezed my hip and I held back a happy sigh. "Hey there. Is Lucy with the others?"

"She found Nora, and now they're running around with Sebastian's mom."

Sebastian laughed. "Those two are thick as thieves, and they're already coming up with baby names." Sebastian swallowed hard as he said it though, and I frowned, before remembering that Sebastian's first love, Nora's mother, had died in childbirth. And now Raven was pregnant. I could only imagine the stress he was under. However, this wasn't the time to bring it up, especially because I didn't know them well. With so many of Kingston's family members in one room, including family members who had married in, so cousins of Kingston's that didn't happen to be cousins of Kane, were all together. It was like a giant block party, complete with champagne, mocktails, and cheese. It also meant that I didn't know everybody here. And while the family members knew each other, people who brought dates or other parts of the family tree didn't know each other. It was just a nice event where people could just relax.

Crew caught my eye, as he scowled, growling on the phone, before stomping out of the building.

Lexington ran after him, and I looked at Kingston who shook his head. "No idea."

"I hope everything's okay," I whispered.

Kingston squeezed my hand, and then we were on the dance floor, everyone else breaking up into groups to dance as well. It was a fast song, and laughter bubbled up, nothing felt too awkward anymore. Instead, it just felt right. After so many things going wrong in the past weeks, the past year, things felt good again.

When the song ended, we were pulled off the dance floor, and Kingston brushed his lips against mine.

"Hey," he breathed, a nervous energy rattling him.

"Hey there. Are you okay?"

He opened his mouth to say something, before Kane came over and tapped him on the shoulder.

"Hey, we need to get Travis in the car, he's passed out drunk, and Aria needs to drive him home. But she can't lift him."

Kingston cursed under his breath, before kissing my temple. "I'll be right back. I promise."

"I'll go with you."

He shook his head, his jaw tense. "No, you don't need to see this."

"Don't kill him," I warned.

"We won't. Promise."

"I'm not going to promise anything about what Crew and Sebastian are going to do," Kane mumbled under his breath, leaving me standing with Phoebe.

"That sucks," Phoebe said after a moment.

"That's succinct. I feel like we should talk with Aria."

"What will we say?" It wasn't as if we had a right to do so or knew what was going on.

"Tell her that we love her, and we don't know what to do for her. Because we're worried," Livvy said as she came up to us, and I hadn't realized she'd overheard.

I shook my head. "Maybe she's just trying to help Travis."

"I don't know. But it hurts to see. And that's why

it's hard to trust most people." Livvy sipped her drink again, before being called over by her parents.

My phone buzzed at that moment, and I looked down at the readout, cursing when I needed to answer it. "I'll be right back."

"Everything okay?" Phoebe asked, worry in her tone.

"I don't know," I answered, a little worried. "Trix? What's going on?"

"The entire liquor distributor just canceled. They had a roof collapse, and they lost it all. I don't know what to do. I can't handle this myself. And there's that huge event tomorrow, and they need us, and now we don't have anything for them." Trix went on and on, her voice going high-pitched, and while my heart raced, panic settling over me, I pushed it aside because this was my job. I had to handle it.

"Where are you?"

"I'm at the event space, setting up."

I frowned, confused. "You're supposed to be home right now. You don't have to work this late, Trix."

"I was running behind. Now I'm glad that I'm here. I have things to do."

I held back a curse because she was correct. I just hated that she was alone in this for the time being. "Okay. I'll head out to you."

"Don't. You're supposed to be celebrating with your boyfriend tonight."

"And you need my help. This is my business. I'm going to help. I'm going to be there."

"I want to say no, but I need your help. I can't handle this on my own."

"We'll handle it together. I'll be there in twenty minutes."

"I'm so sorry."

"It's not your fault."

We said our goodbyes and ended the call, as Phoebe raised her brows at me. "I heard most of that. A roof collapse? Is everyone okay?"

"Trix said no one was in the building at the time so there are no injuries. Just a mess and broken inventory. I have no idea what I'm going to do, but I need to go handle it." I looked across the dance floor, and around the room, but I couldn't see Kingston. "Can you tell Kingston what happened? I'll call him when I get to the place, but I need to go now."

"Okay. I'll do that. Do you want one of us to go with you?"

"No, I'll be fine. Just let Kingston know? I hate leaving him like this." We needed to talk about so many things, but right now I needed to help Trix and my business.

"He'll understand. Knowing him, he'll probably just show up to help out. In fact, if you need any of the Montgomerys, we'll be there."

My heart swelled, because I knew she was right. She would be there. I gave her a quick hug, then went to grab my bag, before running to my car. I had parked on the other side of the building from where Aria's car was, so I didn't even see the others, and I didn't get to say goodbye to anyone else. I made my way down the road, surprised to see that the closer I got to town, the icier the roads were getting. Apparently, the storm was hitting faster than I thought. Once I got to a safe place, I texted Phoebe to let her know so everyone was aware of everything that was going on. Though I was sure that somebody was watching the weather. I put on my windshield wipers as it began to rain, annoyed about mostly everything at this moment. I wanted to be relaxing, I wanted to just be with Kingston. But instead, I was dealing with this.

But this was fine. I was professional, and I would be fine.

Lights came around the bend, blinding me since they had their brights on. I squinted, trying to see the road, as they swerved into my lane, most likely catching on ice. Heart racing, I gripped the steering wheel and pumped the brakes like I was taught, my father's voice echoing in my ears, but it didn't work. There was nothing for my tires to latch on to, the ice underneath spinning me in circles. We were on a large stretch of road, the mountains behind us, fields and a lake nearby, but without streetlights, I couldn't tell, and then everything happened at once.

The sound of metal against metal, my own scream, and then it was as if time stood still, my car careening off of the road down the grass and fields, and at the last moment, my headlights shone on water, and I slammed on the brakes, trying to stop.

But it was too late.

And it was all I could do not to scream louder, as my car slammed right into the icy lake, and the front wheels began to sink.

"You're okay, you're okay," I kept saying to myself, knowing that I wasn't okay. Words came to me in short bursts as everything happened at once.

I was still conscious. I would be fine. I just needed to get out of this car. I went for the door handle, but it wouldn't open. The driver had barely grazed my side of the car, but it was enough to have screwed up the door.

Hands shaking, water beginning to fill the bottom of my car, I kept working on the door latch, but it didn't budge. I was sinking in an icy lake, and nobody knew where I was.

I pushed and I shoved, and I finally let the tears fall.

18

KINGSTON

"I still can't believe that Aria wants to be with that guy "

I reached out and squeezed Crew's shoulder, just as angry as he was. "There's nothing you can do. She knows who he is, and she still wants to try to fix him. But I really hate that guy."

"You're not the only one who hates him." Sebastian pinched the bridge of his nose, thinking. "I need to go talk to my dad. At least…I just need to see him."

"I can't deal with this right now, not with Raven… shit. Aria won't listen to me." And with that, Aria's twin walked away, leaving Crew and me to deal with the mess.

"So Travis is just going to sleep in the car while we wait until Aria leaves? Seems like a dumbass move."

I shrugged. "Honestly, as long as he's not driving, I don't care."

"I'll keep an eye on him," Crew growled, and I raised a brow as he went over to Aria, the two of them whispering in rushed and hushed tones to one another.

I was done with that for now, and now I just wanted to get to Claire. Trying to tell the woman that you loved that you loved her when everyone was pulling you in a thousand different directions was harder than it should have been.

I made it inside, and looked around the area, watching my family and friends laugh and dance, with some of the children sleeping on shoulders, ready to go home. This was what I loved. This was the family that I had grown up in, and the family that I was always going to be part of. I had known what this feeling was my entire life. I hadn't realized it would be the same and yet so radically different for Claire.

I had been blind because I had been waiting for things to make sense when they weren't supposed to. There wasn't going to be a huge sign over my head saying I love you. There should be, and maybe one day I would make one in bright lights so she would understand that I was a fucking idiot, but for now, it was all I could do not to just run around the damn building in search of the woman that I loved.

"Hey, Kingston," Phoebe said, pulling my attention from my spiraling thoughts.

"Hey, Phoebe. Do you know where Claire is?"

"That's why I wanted to find you. There's a huge issue with one of her distributors. A roof caved in—everyone is fine—but Trix needs help."

"What the hell? Claire's going to go help with a caved-in roof?" I asked, wondering if I had heard correctly.

"No, she's not going to the distributor. She's going to the event hall to help Trix with figuring out a plan B or something. She said she would call you when she got there and call us if she needs help. And I growled at her to make sure that she would do it."

"So she's gone. She just left?" I asked, wondering what the hell was going on. She couldn't just leave. Then again, she needed to. It was work. But hell, she hadn't even said goodbye. Maybe I had screwed up. Well, beyond the obvious.

"When did she leave?" I asked.

"Just a few minutes ago. So we just got a weather alert that the storm's coming in faster, I hope she got down the pass before it got icy. As it is, we're going to have to go the back way to get home. But it's okay, we'll all be fine. We're heading out soon."

Alarms spread through me, even though it didn't make any sense. I just had a bad feeling.

"I'm going to go down the pass and just make sure that she's okay."

"What's wrong, Kingston?" Phoebe asked, not telling me that I was a lunatic for wanting to do that. That should have warned me more than anything.

"I don't know. Just have a bad feeling."

"Do you want me to go with you?" Phoebe asked, as Kane came forward.

"What's going on?"

"Claire left to deal with an emergency at work, and I don't know, with the storm coming in, I just want to get to her. So I'm going to go."

"Do you want us to go with you?" Kane asked, and right then and there, I knew that my family would do anything for me.

Because every single person in this room would have freely dropped everything to help, even if it made no sense that I was following Claire to her place of business, just to make sure that she was okay. And I didn't even know the fucking place. I was just going to drive and hopefully catch up to her.

"Yeah, I'll just go," Crew said as he came from behind me. "Aria snapped at me again, and I'm not in the mood to get yelled at for trying to help. So I'll just help you. I drove in with Kane, so I need a ride anyway."

"We'll just head out, catch up to her."

"Drive safe. I'm sure everything's okay," Phoebe said, but there was worry in her gaze, and now that bad feeling intensified.

We headed out to the car, jumping in quickly without words. Something seemed to be on Crew's mind, so I let him be, as we made our way down the road. It was indeed getting a little icy, but the roads had been prepared with salt, so it wasn't too bad.

At least I didn't think so.

"Are you really worried? Where are we going?"

"Phoebe was going to text us the address, will you check?"

"Yeah, I will. So we're just driving around aimlessly for now?" he asked.

"I just want to catch up to her."

"And tell her that you love her?"

"That, and that she doesn't have to do this alone. Hell, am I insane?"

"Yes, but that's fine."

We drove around the bend, and my heart stopped, everything icing over.

"Oh my God." I didn't slam on the brakes since there was indeed ice, but I pumped them, pulling over to the side of the road.

Claire's car, because it had to be hers, was partway in the lake, tilting forward, and the doors weren't open.

"I'll call 911," Crew called out as we both got out of

the car, running toward Claire. There were skid marks all over the road, and I had a feeling that someone else had been on that road. And from the way that there was a huge dent in the side of Claire's car, someone had hit her, run her off the road, and fucking left. Unless they were in the lake first? I didn't have time to think, I just moved toward Claire.

I ran to the door and tried to pull it open, realizing that most of the front was under water, and now Claire was in the back seat, shoving at the door handle.

"Claire!"

She stared right at me, eyes wide, face pale. "Kingston!"

I could barely hear her over the blood pounding in my ears, as the car began to move faster into the water. It seemed that with both of our jostling, the final wheel slid over the mud, and now the car was plummeting into the lake.

"Crew! Get the glass breaker out of my truck."

"On it!" Crew called out, as I pulled on the door handle, the car nearly fully submerged.

"I'll get you. I love you, Claire, I'll get you!" I was screaming the words now, hoping she could hear me. These were not going to be our last words to each other. I went around the other side, but none of the doors were opening, and then, as she slammed on the rear window with her heel, the entire car submerged.

I hadn't even realized how cold the water was, ignoring everything about the temperature and the fact that I was hip deep in it, until I couldn't see her anymore. I took a deep breath, and submerged myself, trying to get the doors open from this way, but they weren't budging.

I didn't know how much air she would have left. How much water was inside the car. This lake wasn't deep, but it was deep enough to cover a fucking car. I threw myself at the door, but it wouldn't budge. Claire's pale hands were slamming against the glass, and I met her gaze, the fear there, but I wasn't going to let her die. I pressed my feet into the muddy ground, and pushed my way up to the surface, gasping for air. Crew was already there, knee-deep in the water, and tossed me the glass-shattering tool. "Ambulance is on its way. What do you need?"

"Help me get her out." And then I dived again and held onto the door handle. I waved the tool in the water, and Claire moved back, hopefully realizing what I needed to do. I slammed it against the window, and it shattered, water rushing into the car.

I didn't know if I had air, I didn't know where up was or down was, but Crew was by my side, and then Claire's hand was in mine, and I moved. I wasn't quite sure what happened next, as everything moved in slow motion and yet so quickly all at once. As our heads breached the surface, I gasped for air, Claire doing the same, and although our feet could reach the ground, I didn't let her go.

Crew was right by my side, both of us moving toward the embankment, as Claire shivered in my arms.

"You came. How are you here?"

"I didn't want you to go without saying goodbye. And I just had a bad feeling."

Crew coughed near us—his voice as shaky as ours. "I'm going to go get blankets from your trunk. You have them, right?"

I nodded, hoping Crew could see me, because I could only focus on her. "I love you, Claire. I'm so sorry I didn't say it before. But I couldn't find the words. But I love you so fucking much. I was trying to tell you today, not when everything was in jeopardy. I swear to you. I never want to live my life without you, Claire. I love you so fucking much. Please be okay."

Tears filled her eyes, as she shivered, her lips blue. "I love you too, I can't believe you're here. I couldn't get the doors open. They automatically locked, and then they wouldn't unlock. And then whoever ran me off the road seemed to have screwed with my door, as they slammed into me, but I don't know."

I checked her for cuts and bruises and saw a few and cursed.

Crew was there in a moment, wrapping a blanket

around her, then tossing another one to me. "Get warm too. I don't need everyone with hypothermia."

"I thought I was the guy who knew how to handle things in an emergency, turns out it's you," I told Crew, who snorted at me, though I saw the fear there.

"Not just me. Holy hell, Claire, never do that again, okay?"

"I promise. Never again." Her teeth were chattering then, and I held her close, all three of us sitting in the mud as it began to rain ice-cold water droplets over us, and we looked at the man-made lake, and the fact that we couldn't see her fucking car.

"I need to get one of those little glass things for my car." She shivered in my arms again. "Or maybe get a car first?"

"I've got you. I've got you."

Crew just sat next to me, hand on my shoulder, as we sat there, our entire lives feeling as if they had slammed into us all at once, the sound of sirens echoing in the distance.

BY THE TIME we were at the hospital, Claire was sent back, and they wouldn't let me go with her. Even though they had said she had told them that I could go to her room, the staff needed more time with her. We had had to deal with the authorities, and Claire had already given a description of the car though she hadn't really seen it.

"I still can't believe that you just showed up," Hudson said, pacing the hallway as we waited to see Claire.

My stomach tightened thinking about the other option. "I just had a bad feeling. And I wanted to see her."

"It's about damn time that you said that you love her by the way," Hudson said.

"What?" I blinked, trying to keep up with the conversation since my mind was in the room with Claire.

"When they let me back for a second to talk to her, she mentioned that you both said the words; she was sort of rambling. I think she's still in shock."

I shook my head, my heart in my throat. "Of course I love her. I'm just an idiot and it took me a while to say it."

"Of course you're an idiot. You're a guy in love."

"I'm sure there's a movie or something called that."

Hudson's lips quirked. "The kids are with Leif and Brooke, since they had come home early from the party, and my parents are still on a cruise. I can't believe they're on a fucking cruise right now."

"Do they get home soon?"

"It's a month-long cruise. It's one of their bucket list items. So it's hard to get phone calls out to them. But I'll tell them everything."

"A Kingston Montgomery?" one of the orderlies said, and I turned on my heel.

"Yes?"

"Claire would like to see you."

"Okay, I'll be right there." I turned to Hudson. "You okay out here?"

"I'm going to try to get hold of the parents. You go make sure my sister's okay. Thank you though. For saving her life? I could never repay you."

"She's my everything. I don't know what I'd do if I hadn't been there."

We met gazes, both of us swallowing hard, until I finally made my way into Claire's room. She lay there, so small, wrapped in a blanket, and smiled at me.

"I'm fine," she said for what had to be the fifteenth time that hour.

"You might be fine, but I'm not."

Her eyes widened and she looked me over, panic etched on her face. "Did you get checked out?"

"I wasn't in the water for as long as you."

"Mr. Montgomery?" one of the nurses cut in, and I shook my head.

"Claire first. I'm okay. Promise."

I had changed into scrubs, and looked ridiculous,

but I didn't care. I just needed to make sure Claire was okay. Soon we were left alone, and I cupped her face with my hands.

"Are you truly okay?"

She nodded, her gaze on mine. "Minor hypothermia and a few cuts and bruises. But I'm very, very lucky."

My body shuddered thinking about it. "I still can't believe I was on the road."

"Whatever fate or gods pushed you toward that, I'm forever grateful."

I kissed the top of her head and tried not to fall right there with her right in front of me. "Damn straight."

"So, you love me?" she whispered.

"Fuck yes." When she laughed, I knew I had said the right thing. "I haven't felt this way before and I didn't know what it meant. But I knew I needed to say something."

"I'm not great at saying things either. As is evidenced by how long it took me to tell you anything about what I felt."

"I was worried about you, and I wanted to come see you, so I was going to help at your work, completely unasked, completely over the top. I never expected the accident. Hell. I never expected you." I paused, shaking my head. "I'm not great at this."

"Like I am?" she said with a laugh.

"I know I can't be the one that fixes everything. I

know that. But I want to be. I want to be the one who can do it all. But in the end, I know I just need to try. To be with you."

"You saved me, you know."

"You were saving yourself," I said truthfully. "You would've gotten out."

"Maybe. But how about we just try to save each other, and not keep a tally. Because I love you. I should have said it before. Even without knowing that you would say it as well. I love you. And I'm so glad that we got stuck in a snowstorm."

"Always. But how about no more natural disasters?" I asked with a laugh.

"Deal." And when I kissed her again, everything felt right. Finally.

"**A** carriage? Yes, we could totally handle that. Yes, I have a guy."

I leaned against the doorway, crossing my hands over my chest as I watched Claire fold laundry while on her phone, explaining that she had a guy with a horse-drawn carriage.

This was something I needed to investigate.

I had tried to go in there and help fold the laundry earlier, and she had smacked my hand and told me that it was my day off from doing chores. Considering it was her house. Well, she didn't have to know that I had already taken out the trash, cleaned the gutters, and was going to work on doing some touch-ups on the paint around the place once I found her paint-brushes. I knew she had them because she had mentioned it was on her to-do list for later that day, so I would just get started. Claire had done laundry, as well as a few other things around the house that had taken her most of the morning while she was on the phone working. I didn't know how she could do seventeen things at once. I usually needed to be focused on one thing at a time unless I was on the job and aware of our surroundings. That was inherent. But Claire could do seven things at once while still having a conversation.

"No problem. I will send you an email with all the quotes and see what we can do. And you're right, there's a few other things that we should handle, but we can do that in person after the first?" She smiled, shaking her hips as she worked, and my gaze went straight to that action. My cock hardening and tenting my gray sweatpants.

"Yes, happy holidays to you. And don't worry. I'm here for you." She shook again, and I held back an audible groan. "Yes, have a great day. Goodbye." And then Claire turned around to end the call and met my gaze. She screamed loudly, dropping the set of clean panties in her hands, and pressed her fist to her heart.

"I didn't know you were watching me. Stalker much?"

I snorted, then leaned forward, brushing my lips against hers.

"I was just watching you dance. I can't help it. You do things to me."

"Well. I can see that." She pointed to my erection, and I shrugged, my cock bobbing along with the movement.

"You can't blame me. You were bending over. And dancing."

"And you're not wearing underwear, are you?"

"That's the point of gray sweatpants. I'm supposed to seduce you with my VPL."

"Where did you even learn that word?" she asked with a laugh.

"I know things. I'm very savvy."

"And I do not even want to know," she said with a laugh. "And what have you been doing with that VPL of yours?" she asked, raising both brows. She was so cute because she couldn't raise one at a time, and it kept bugging her that so many in her life could.

"I'm not going to sit on my ass while you're working and cleaning your house."

"But it's your day off."

"And? Let me help. I like doing things with you. I love you."

It was never going to get old hearing those words coming from my mouth. I grew up knowing that love and happiness were something that you could attain. I grew up in a household where my family loved me, and

I watched healthy relationships bloom around me day in and day out. I always assumed that one day I would find that one person, and I would know when it happened. I would immediately find myself on a path that I had been prepared for because of my connections.

I hadn't realized that I was such a damn idiot for so long.

"I love you too. It scares me a little bit how much I do."

I leaned forward, brushing my fingers along her jawbone. "Why are you scared? You shouldn't be."

"I'm not scared of you. Or even of us. I just didn't realize I could feel like this. I spent so long trying not to feel everything because I was so scared and I didn't realize that I could have this."

I reached down and handed her the scrap of panties, and she rolled her eyes before throwing them back in the washer. "Yes, laundry on the floor, us in sweats, and you doing my housework even though I asked you not to."

"I even cleaned your gutters."

"You were on a ladder without me? Kingston."

"There were no dogs around to push me off the ladder. I was fine."

"Well at least you're getting over that fear. I feel like maybe I should have told you a long time ago that I liked you. But we're not in high school, and I wasn't going to wait for you to see me. I just hid in myself. And how silly was that?"

I clucked my tongue, and then ran my fingers down her arms before grasping her hands in mine. "I'm just annoyed that a bear literally walked past us, and while my cousin and Phoebe were safe in the car, I didn't realize that the woman of my dreams was hiding in that bathroom."

"Oh yes, in a state park bathroom, so sexy."

"You are fucking sexy."

"To be honest, I'm glad that we became friends. And that I didn't have to stress myself out for too long over if you would see me or not."

"I should have seen you."

"We weren't ready yet. And hey, now we don't have to think about it because you're stuck with me. I am very sorry."

"I'm not sorry at all."

"Did you really clean the gutters?"

"Yep. That's one less thing on your to-do list. I was looking for paintbrushes to work on touching up the trim."

"You're ridiculous." I wrapped my arms around her, as she snuggled into my chest. She smelled so damn good, and I couldn't help but let my hands wander, cupping her ass. Even though it was almost New Year's, snow all around, she was wearing tiny little shorts under one of my sweatshirts. And as I probed underneath the shorts just to see, I grinned. "You're not wearing any underwear either."

"Kingston Montgomery. We have to do work before we head out to your parents' house for dinner. Though this does seem like it's an awfully big event."

I squeezed her ass, and she laughed.

"I'm pretty sure that nearly dying and then coming together in the hospital room is the Montgomery rite of passage to become family. So you're stuck with me. And your family's coming over for dinner too."

"Just Hudson and the kids. My parents are off on their cruise."

"Well, Hudson and the kids are already part of the Montgomery way of life, so they're going to get doubly so."

"This doesn't feel real."

I brushed my lips against hers again, and she sighed into me.

"Oh, I'm pretty sure it's real. But let's check." And so without giving her any warning, I gripped her by the hips, and lifted her so she sat on the dryer. When she let out a squeak, I pressed a few buttons, and the dryer began to tumble.

Her eyes widened, and I slid in between her legs.

"Kingston. I wasn't done. There's still wet laundry in the washer."

"We'll deal with the laundry in a second. Let's just see how this whole tumbling thing works. I've never tried it."

"Well, sitting on a dryer's mostly a girl thing."

I raised that single brow and she scowled at me.

"You've gotten yourself off on a dryer before. And I thought you were the sweet and innocent one."

She reached down and gripped me underneath the band of my sweats.

"Oh, we can see exactly who's the innocent one here."

I kissed her with everything that I had, both of us groaning into one another. It took a bit of maneuvering, and then her shorts were off, and my hands were underneath the sweatshirt, cupping her breasts.

"Kingston. I need you."

"I've got you," I growled. "I've got you." And as I shoved my sweatpants down past my knees, I slid deep inside her. We both groaned, the dryer making her move on my dick without me even trying, and both of us laughed a bit, and then we were moving with abandon, with Claire leaning back to hold onto the edge of the dryer, and me thrusting into her as the dryer moved quickly. The warmth added to the sensation, and we laughed, continued to find each other, and when she came, I followed, unable to hold back any longer.

"Well damn," I whispered. "I wonder what would happen if we used permanent press?"

"Maybe next time. My ass is getting hot."

I immediately pulled her off the dryer, both of us laughing, and then I kissed her again, needing her close.

"You know I never expected you. I know I keep saying that. But I didn't. I thought you were just ignoring me all those months because I fucked up."

"You didn't fuck up. And I was ignoring you because...well, I was in my own head. For obvious reasons. And because you saw me bleeding out on the floor and helpless. I thought I loved you, but I really just loved the idea of you. And that crush just made everything a little twisted in my brain. But I love you. And I guess us getting trapped in a cabin in the woods was the best thing ever."

"I'm going to be forever grateful for old fashioneds, snow, and you riding my dick."

"You should put that on a card. It would sell millions."

"I just might do that. The next Montgomery dynasty?" I pressed a hard kiss to her lips, and then we laughed as we cleaned up, both of us taking our time in the shower.

That of course meant we were late to the dinner, and Claire's brother gave me a knowing look as we showed up.

"Well, I see you had a fun day."

"Stop it," Claire said as she kissed her brother's cheeks, and then held out her arms for her niece and nephew. They tumbled on top of her, as my brothers came through, both of them laughing at the sight.

"It's nice not to be the youngest anymore," Oliver said, and Logan snorted.

"You still act younger." They shoved at each other, as my mom came through and shook her head at them.

"They never really grow out of it," she said dryly to Hudson, and Hudson sighed.

"So I hear."

"We have a straggler for dinner if that's okay," Mom said, and I frowned as Ford came in.

"Hey. I came in with news, and now I get dinner. Greer and Noah are on date night, so now I don't have to eat leftovers."

"Like either one of them would ever let you just have leftovers on their date night," Lincoln said with a sigh. "Plus I know you know how to cook."

"Fine, fine. They're amazing and didn't leave me alone. I'm blessed."

"What's wrong?" Claire asked, as she came back, her hand coming into mine.

"Yeah, what's up, Ford?"

Hudson cleared his throat and looked at the twins. "Hey, can you go upstairs and go get that present you have for your aunt? We'll let you know when you can come down."

"I hate not being an adult," Claire's nephew said as Claire's niece just sighed and the two left the room.

I frowned at Ford, confused. "We were at work all day yesterday, and I've had my phone on me. What's up?"

"The officer's going to call you tomorrow, but I just wanted to make sure that you knew that they found the car."

Claire stiffened next to me, and I wrapped my arm around her. Hudson came closer, a scowl on his face.

"What do you mean they found the car?"

In the weeks since the accident, they had been searching for the driver and car that had run Claire off the road and almost killed her. But they hadn't found it. The lack of evidence, and the snowstorm had pushed everything behind. Then there had been a giant pileup on the highway, as well as a double homicide in the same area, and while it had nothing to do with Claire's accident, it did pull focus.

But not for us, never for us.

"They found the car abandoned, about ten miles outside of Westminster."

I blinked. "All the way down there?"

He nodded. "Yes. It made it all the way down there,

and there was clear evidence that it was the car that hit Claire."

"What happened to the driver?" Claire asked, her voice low.

Ford shook his head. "Turns out he turned himself in this morning."

My jaw dropped as Claire gasped. "Just like that?" I asked, anger rising. "After all this time?"

"It was a kid, Claire," Ford said, speaking directly to her and wisely ignoring my anger. "The cops are going to call you in the morning because they were still working through things. I just have a buddy that was keeping me in the loop because we've been helping him with another case. That's the only reason I know now. And I literally just found out. It was a kid. Some seventeen-year-old who had been drinking cheap booze and didn't realize what he was doing. He stole his dad's car, and then kept driving because he was so damn scared. And when they found the car, the kid wasn't home, but the dad was. I don't know the whole story, but the kid showed up at the precinct, and told them everything. I don't know what's going to happen to him, it's not going to be good. He's seventeen, they can treat him like an adult. But he was scared shitless."

"He almost killed Claire," I growled.

Claire patted my chest, her voice soft when she spoke. "But I'm fine. How scary for that kid though?"

"Don't...don't pity him," I snapped.

"I'm with Kingston on this," Hudson agreed.

"I can be angry with him later. I've been angry with whoever this imaginary person was this entire time. But right now, I'm just sad. His entire life has changed, and I'm fine. Yes, I was scared, but we've been through worse. Every single person in this room has been through worse. Which is terrifying considering what happened. But we're okay, and we're in this new year, and I just want good things to happen. So let's have this family dinner which has been stressing me out all day because it's a meet the parents thing even though I know you guys, and well, here I am. Panicking over this. But I love all of you. Every single person in this room. So let's just deal with it tomorrow. Because I'm okay." She repeated, looking at me, "I'm okay."

I sighed, and wrapped my arms around her, as I saw out of the corner of my eye my mom wiping tears from her face. "Well, I always wanted a daughter. I'm glad that I have you."

"Mom," I whispered.

"Oh shush. I'm not pushing you into marriage or defining your relationship—I'm adopting her. It's going to get a little weird later with the paperwork, but she's mine now. I'm sorry."

I laughed, as my mom took Claire from me, and

Ethan held me close. "I love you, son. Don't be angry. You'll deal with it later."

I met Ford's gaze, and he nodded, and I knew we would.

My job was protecting people. And finding ways for them to protect themselves. The fact that Claire was able to find that space in order to say what she did? She was so much stronger than any of us. And maybe, just maybe, I hadn't failed as many times as I thought. So we would deal with the future together, all of us. We would deal with the driver, with the next calamity that came to the Montgomerys, and anything that the world threw at us.

Claire looked over her shoulder and winked at me, and I lifted my chin, before I went over to her, my family surrounding me.

One night had changed everything, but in the end, I got the girl.

I had finally fallen for the girl who had always been there.

And it was about damn time.

20

CLAIRE

Dear Diary,

I haven't written in this journal since right after the attack and now I realize that maybe that was for the best. I didn't need to show you who I was when I didn't know who that person could be.

But now I'm better.

And not because I fell in love with Kingston Montgomery.

The real Kingston Montgomery.

Yes, he was a part of it but he wasn't all of it.

I found that knowing what I wanted meant

I had to fight for it—even if fighting myself was part of the problem.

I'm no longer the girl lying on the floor, covered in her own blood.

I'm no longer the girl who can't fight back.

I'm no longer the girl who can't forgive.

I'm alive. I'm free. And I'm in love with myself.

And that love took far longer than I care to admit.

And yes, I love Kingston Montgomery.

Maybe I should go back and write about our first night...but no...that's just for me.

Finally.

-Claire

I could have sworn the sheet rock rumbled, as the pictures on the wall shuddered.

"Please. I can't...please."

I shut her up with my mouth, one hand sliding up her thigh, pushing her dress out of the way so I could get more of her skin. The other hand slid up her arm and pinned it above her head, fingers tangling with one another.

My mouth crushed down on hers, both of us fighting for control, driving deep within one another.

My hand slid between her legs, over her panties, and cupped her.

"Oh," she moaned, and I continued to kiss her, trailing my mouth down her jaw, over her neck. When my fingers tugged her panties to the side, my fingers grew wet just by a bare brush.

"So fucking wet for me. You want this. You're a dirty girl, aren't you?"

"Stop talking and make me come."

I let go of her hand, and slid that hand right over her throat, my thumb sliding along her neck.

"Oh, it's like that, is it?"

Those piercing blue eyes narrowed.

"Always."

I ignored the barb, and then with my gaze on hers, speared her with two fingers. She drenched my hand, my thumb pressing along her clit as she rocked her hips.

"That's it, be a good little girl and ride my hand."

"Don't call me that," she bit out, before I slid my thumb into her mouth, forcing her to lick and suck.

"Fine."

And that was right anyway. Because she knew I only said the words to get a rise out of her. I never knew what I was saying when it came to her. Only that wasn't something I was going to say.

No. We would keep this distance, as I finger-fucked her, and she drenched my hand as if she couldn't hold back any longer.

And when she came, clamping down at my fingers, I kept moving, the sounds of sex filling the hallway.

There was nothing more I could do, nothing more that I could say. So I pulled my fingers out of her, and then used both hands to grip her hips.

"More?" I asked.

No matter how much I wanted to pretend that this meant nothing, something told me this was a lie. But no, this was just sex. A quick fuck, a hard one. She could debase me, call me names, and I would do just the same for her.

Because it didn't matter.

Nothing mattered.

"I just...I don't want to think." She stared up at me with wide eyes and I knew what she needed—what she refused or couldn't voice.

I nodded, understanding, then undid my jeans with one hand, keeping my mouth on hers. When we pulled away, and I slid the condom over my length, I couldn't help but take a moment to step back, and stare at the beauty of her.

I had already pulled down her dress, so her breasts were bare, her nipples hard little points already swollen from my mouth from before. Half of her dress was slid to the side, the other half pushed up. Her panties were a damp mess shoved to the side, and I wanted her. Needed her.

I kissed her again, hating myself. And then I slammed deep inside her. One thrust, one motion, and she was screaming my name, pulsating around my cock as she came, and I moved.

The picture frames continued to bash against the wall as I fucked her hard against it. There was nothing more I could do, just this.

I needed her. Needed her more than the air I breathed. But I knew it had to be only for sex. It was what we were good for.

It wasn't as if I really wanted more.

And when I finally came, pinning her to the wall, her fingernails dug into my shoulders, and I kept her to me, hips against hips, buried balls deep. Both of our breaths came in pants, as we tried to calm our hearts, but there was nothing more I could do. Nothing more I could say.

I pulled out of her and ditched the condom in the trash nearby. She righted herself, not meeting my gaze, and I ignored it.

Because this was just a mistake.

Just like it had been before.

"So, are we going to talk about it?" I asked, my voice a growl. I didn't mean for the biting tone. I didn't *mean* to say anything. But I was so damn tired.

Aria Montgomery shook her head and wiped a tear from her cheek.

I cursed under my breath, and moved closer, wiping the second tear with my thumb. Nothing made sense anymore. It couldn't. I had done that. Doing what both of us had wanted. Playing a game. And I had left that tear. I hated the names. But the names were doing what we were good at. Playing a game.

"I can't," she whispered, her voice breaking.

I tucked myself back into my pants and swallowed hard. "Because you love him. Even with all he's done, you love him."

She met my gaze again, those blue Montgomery eyes staring daggers into my soul. "No, I... I know I can't love him. And I don't really."

"Aria. You can lie to yourself every day. But you don't get to lie to me. Not when we play games here. We can play games when I'm deep inside you, but you don't get to play games here."

"I loved the idea of him...but with this..." Her voice trailed off and she didn't look at me. I knew there was more going on in that brilliant mind of hers than this moment. And I wasn't part of it. We'd both taken advantage. Just like always. "This can't happen again."

I nodded tightly, knowing that all good things, even how dirty and manipulative they could be, had to come to an end.

"Fine."

"You were with Daisy. My best friend. My cousin."

And here it came—the rationalization. It surprised me it had taken her this long to find the road she wanted to go down when it came to pushing me away.

Too bad I'd be the one walking—even if she didn't realize it. "Well, Daisy's not my cousin because that would have been wrong, but she is my best friend. I'm allowed to fuck other people you know."

Aria looked like I had hit her, and I could have rightly hit myself.

"Aria..."

She shook her head. "I have to go."

I looked down at her disheveled dress and hair and didn't bother to tell her that she could get cleaned up. Because if she stayed, we'd fuck again, and then she would do the worst thing ever, and fall asleep in my arms.

And that's not what we did.

"Fine. Go. But we're done—you and me. I'm done being the one that you run to when things get hard because you know I don't ask questions."

Aria lifted her chin then, looking like the Montgomery I knew. So fierce, so passionate. So not mine. "All you do is ask questions, Crew. I'm the one that never has the answers. And you're the one that never lets me ask *mine*." And when another tear fell, and another, I didn't bother to wipe them away. Instead, she turned and left, picking up her purse and closing the door quietly behind her.

Aria Montgomery didn't want to cause a scene. She wouldn't slam the door. Instead, she would leave, and once again I watched the woman that I pretended not to love run away.

Next in the Montgomery Ink Legacy series:
Aria and Crew keep a secret in Accidentally Forever

IF YOU'D LIKE TO READ A BONUS SCENE:
CHECK OUT THIS SPECIAL EPILOGUE!

A NOTE FROM CARRIE ANN RYAN

Thank you so much for reading **ONE NIGHT WITH YOU!**

Writing Kingston and Claire's story was one of those things that gave me so much joy. Yes, their road was rocky, but they deserved their HEA so freaking much. I love writing the Montgomerys. They are honestly like coming home and watching the child of one of the Montgomery triads all grown up is like a little Easter egg for myself and those who have followed along for years.

The next book in the series is going to be explosive. Just saying. Crew and Aria are ready to change a few things in Accidentally Forever!

And Livvy will get her story. Don't worry.

Oh…and Hudson? Hmm….

And because I knew I needed to tell the story...The Cages get their own romances in The Cage Family, starting with The Forever Rule !

The Montgomery Ink Legacy Series:
    Book 1: Bittersweet Promises (Leif & Brooke)
    Book 2: At First Meet (Nick & Lake)
    Book 2.5: Happily Ever Never (May & Leo)
    Book 3: Longtime Crush (Sebastian & Raven)
    Book 4: Best Friend Temptation (Noah, Ford, and Greer)
    Book 4.5: Happily Ever Maybe (Jennifer & Gus)
    Book 5: Last First Kiss (Daisy & Hugh)
    Book 6: His Second Chance (Kane & Phoebe)
    Book 7: One Night with You (Kingston & Claire)
    Book 8: Accidentally Forever (Crew & Aria)
    Book 9: Last Chance Seduction (Lexington & Mercy)

Next in the Montgomery Ink Legacy series:
Aria and Crew keep a secret in Accidentally Forever

IF YOU'D LIKE TO READ A BONUS SCENE:
CHECK OUT THIS SPECIAL EPILOGUE!

If you want to make sure you know what's coming next from me, you can sign up for my newsletter at www. CarrieAnnRyan.com; follow me on twitter at

@CarrieAnnRyan, or like my Facebook page. I also have a Facebook Fan Club where we have trivia, chats, and other goodies. You guys are the reason I get to do what I do and I thank you.

Make sure you're signed up for my MAILING LIST so you can know when the next releases are available as well as find giveaways and FREE READS.

Happy Reading!

ALSO FROM CARRIE ANN RYAN

The Montgomery Ink Legacy Series:

Book 1: Bittersweet Promises (Leif & Brooke)

Book 2: At First Meet (Nick & Lake)

Book 2.5: Happily Ever Never (May & Leo)

Book 3: Longtime Crush (Sebastian & Raven)

Book 4: Best Friend Temptation (Noah, Ford, and Greer)

Book 4.5: Happily Ever Maybe (Jennifer & Gus)

Book 5: Last First Kiss (Daisy & Hugh)

Book 6: His Second Chance (Kane & Phoebe)

Book 7: One Night with You (Kingston & Claire)

Book 8: Accidentally Forever (Crew & Aria)

Book 9: Last Chance Seduction (Lexington & Mercy)

The Wilder Brothers Series:

Book 1: One Way Back to Me (Eli & Alexis)

Book 2: Always the One for Me (Evan & Kendall)

Book 3: The Path to You (Everett & Bethany)

Book 4: Coming Home for Us (Elijah & Maddie)

Book 5: Stay Here With Me (East & Lark)

Book 6: Finding the Road to Us (Elliot, Trace, and Sidney)

Book 7: Moments for You (Ridge & Aurora)

Book 7.5: A Wilder Wedding (Amos & Naomi)

Book 8: Forever For Us (Wyatt & Ava)

Book 9: Pieces of Me (Gabriel & Briar)

Book 10: Endlessly Yours (Brooks & Rory)

The Cage Family

Book 1: The Forever Rule (Aston & Blakely)

Book 2: An Unexpected Everything (Isabella & Weston)

Book 3: If You Were Mine (Dorian & Harper)

The First Time Series:

Book 1: Good Time Boyfriend (Heath & Devney)

Book 2: Last Minute Fiancé (Luca & Addison)

Book 3: Second Chance Husband (August & Paisley)

The Montgomery Ink: Fort Collins Series:

Book 1: Inked Persuasion (Jacob & Annabelle)

Book 2: Inked Obsession (Beckett & Eliza)

Book 3: Inked Devotion (Benjamin & Brenna)

Book 3.5: Nothing But Ink (Clay & Riggs)

Book 4: Inked Craving (Lee & Paige)

Book 5: Inked Temptation (Archer & Killian)

The Montgomery Ink: Boulder Series:

Book 1: Wrapped in Ink (Liam & Arden)

Book 2: Sated in Ink (Ethan, Lincoln, and Holland)

Book 3: Embraced in Ink (Bristol & Marcus)

Book 3: Moments in Ink (Zia & Meredith)

Book 4: Seduced in Ink (Aaron & Madison)

Book 4.5: Captured in Ink (Julia, Ronin, & Kincaid)

Book 4.7: Inked Fantasy (Secret ??)

Book 4.8: A Very Montgomery Christmas (The Entire Boulder Family)

Montgomery Ink: Colorado Springs

Book 1: Fallen Ink (Adrienne & Mace)

Book 2: Restless Ink (Thea & Dimitri)

Book 2.5: Ashes to Ink (Abby & Ryan)

Book 3: Jagged Ink (Roxie & Carter)

Book 3.5: Ink by Numbers (Landon & Kaylee)

Montgomery Ink Denver:

Book 0.5: Ink Inspired (Shep & Shea)

Book 0.6: Ink Reunited (Sassy, Rare, and Ian)

Book 1: Delicate Ink (Austin & Sierra)

Book 1.5: <u>Forever Ink</u> (Callie & Morgan)

Book 2: <u>Tempting Boundaries</u> (Decker and Miranda)

Book 3: <u>Harder than Words</u> (Meghan & Luc)

Book 3.5: <u>Finally Found You</u> (Mason & Presley)

Book 4: <u>Written in Ink</u> (Griffin & Autumn)

Book 4.5: <u>Hidden Ink</u> (Hailey & Sloane)

Book 5: <u>Ink Enduring</u> (Maya, Jake, and Border)

Book 6: <u>Ink Exposed</u> (Alex & Tabby)

Book 6.5: <u>Adoring Ink</u> (Holly & Brody)

Book 6.6: <u>Love, Honor, & Ink</u> (Arianna & Harper)

Book 7: <u>Inked Expressions</u> (Storm & Everly)

Book 7.3: <u>Dropout</u> (Grayson & Kate)

Book 7.5: <u>Executive Ink</u> (Jax & Ashlynn)

Book 8: <u>Inked Memories</u> (Wes & Jillian)

Book 8.5: <u>Inked Nights</u> (Derek & Olivia)

Book 8.7: <u>Second Chance Ink</u> (Brandon & Lauren)

Book 8.5: Montgomery Midnight Kisses (Alex & Tabby Bonus(

Bonus: Inked Kingdom (Stone & Sarina)

The On My Own Series:

Book 0.5: My First Glance

Book 1: My One Night (Dillon & Elise)

Book 2: My Rebound (Pacey & Mackenzie)

Book 3: My Next Play (Miles & Nessa)

Book 4: My Bad Decisions (Tanner & Natalie)

The Promise Me Series:

Book 1: Forever Only Once (Cross & Hazel)

Book 2: From That Moment (Prior & Paris)

Book 3: Far From Destined (Macon & Dakota)

Book 4: From Our First (Nate & Myra)

The Less Than Series:

Book 1: Breathless With Her (Devin & Erin)

Book 2: Reckless With You (Tucker & Amelia)

Book 3: Shameless With Him (Caleb & Zoey)

The Fractured Connections Series:

Book 1: Breaking Without You (Cameron & Violet)

Book 2: Shouldn't Have You (Brendon & Harmony)

Book 3: Falling With You (Aiden & Sienna)

Book 4: Taken With You (Beckham & Meadow)

The Whiskey and Lies Series:

Book 1: Whiskey Secrets (Dare & Kenzie)

Book 2: Whiskey Reveals (Fox & Melody)

Book 3: Whiskey Undone (Loch & Ainsley)

The Gallagher Brothers Series:

Book 1: Love Restored (Graham & Blake)

Book 2: Passion Restored (Owen & Liz)

Book 3: Hope Restored (Murphy & Tessa)

The Ravenwood Coven Series:

Book 1: Dawn Unearthed

Book 2: Dusk Unveiled

Book 3: Evernight Unleashed

The Aspen Pack Series:

Book 1: Etched in Honor

Book 2: Hunted in Darkness

Book 3: Mated in Chaos

Book 4: Harbored in Silence

Book 5: Marked in Flames

The Talon Pack:

Book 1: Tattered Loyalties

Book 2: An Alpha's Choice

Book 3: Mated in Mist

Book 4: Wolf Betrayed

Book 5: Fractured Silence

Book 6: Destiny Disgraced

Book 7: Eternal Mourning

Book 8: Strength Enduring

Book 9: Forever Broken

Book 10: Mated in Darkness

Book 11: Fated in Winter

Redwood Pack Series:

Book 1: An Alpha's Path

Book 2: <u>A Taste for a Mate</u>
Book 3: <u>Trinity Bound</u>
Book 3.5: <u>A Night Away</u>
Book 4: <u>Enforcer's Redemption</u>
Book 4.5: <u>Blurred Expectations</u>
Book 4.7: <u>Forgiveness</u>
Book 5: <u>Shattered Emotions</u>
Book 6: <u>Hidden Destiny</u>
Book 6.5: <u>A Beta's Haven</u>
Book 7: <u>Fighting Fate</u>
Book 7.5: <u>Loving the Omega</u>
Book 7.7: <u>The Hunted Heart</u>
Book 8: <u>Wicked Wolf</u>

The Elements of Five Series:
Book 1: From Breath and Ruin
Book 2: From Flame and Ash
Book 3: From Spirit and Binding
Book 4: From Shadow and Silence

Dante's Circle Series:
Book 1: <u>Dust of My Wings</u>
Book 2: <u>Her Warriors' Three Wishes</u>
Book 3: <u>An Unlucky Moon</u>
Book 3.5: <u>His Choice</u>
Book 4: <u>Tangled Innocence</u>
Book 5: <u>Fierce Enchantment</u>

Book 6: <u>An Immortal's Song</u>

Book 7: <u>Prowled Darkness</u>

Book 8: Dante's Circle Reborn

Holiday, Montana Series:

Book 1: <u>Charmed Spirits</u>

Book 2: <u>Santa's Executive</u>

Book 3: <u>Finding Abigail</u>

Book 4: <u>Her Lucky Love</u>

Book 5: Dreams of Ivory

The Branded Pack Series:

(Written with Alexandra Ivy)

Book 1: <u>Stolen and Forgiven</u>

Book 2: <u>Abandoned and Unseen</u>

Book 3: <u>Buried and Shadowed</u>

ABOUT THE AUTHOR

Carrie Ann Ryan is the New York Times and USA Today bestselling author of contemporary, paranormal, and young adult romance. Her works include the Montgomery Ink, Redwood Pack, Fractured Connections, and Elements of Five series, which have sold over 3.0 million books worldwide. She started writing while in graduate school for her advanced degree in chemistry and hasn't stopped since. Carrie Ann has written over seventy-five novels and novellas with more in the works. When she's not losing herself in her emotional and action-packed worlds, she's reading as much as she can while wrangling her clowder of cats who have more followers than she does.

www.CarrieAnnRyan.com

www.ingramcontent.com/pod-product-compliance
Lightning Source LLC
Chambersburg PA
CBHW011146100726
47899CB00010B/3184